SPY GAMES

SPY GAMES

JONATHAN SCANLAN SERIES
BOOK 3

BARRY SOLLOWAY

BOOK 3 OF THE JONATHAN SCANLAN SERIES

SPY GAMES

BARRY SOLLOWAY

Library of Congress Control Number: 2026908147
Paperback ISBN: 979-8-9930967-4-2
Digital Book ISBN: 979-8-9930967-5-9

For Amanda and Kate

CHAPTER 1

The late model Ford Explorer rolled to a stop on a quiet street in Flower Mound, Texas, a middle-class suburb outside of Dallas. It was after 1:00 a.m., and no lights were on in the homes in the area. The three men in the SUV sat for several moments before stepping out of the vehicle, listening and looking for any movement on the street.

Streetlights offered some visibility, but the men moved in the shadows as they approached the home on Abbey Lane. All were wearing black clothing, and their faces were obscured by ski masks.

One of the men removed a set of picks, but found them unnecessary, as the front door was unlocked. They slid into the house noiselessly. They paused as they glanced around the entry and nearby living room, using night vision goggles. The two-story home possessed a conventional floorplan, with living areas downstairs and bedrooms on the second floor.

They moved quietly up the stairs. Two of the men approached the master bedroom while the third man moved to a smaller bedroom down the hall. They eased the bedroom doors open and stepped into the rooms.

In the master bedroom Raymond Wu was asleep on the left side of the bed, while his wife, Teresa was on the right. The two men in black moved to each side of the bed and, with quick, brutal blows, killed the sleeping couple.

The third man stepped to the side of the bed and studied the sleeping boy. Without hesitation he clubbed, Joseph Wu, the sleeping teenager.

He lifted the unconscious boy from the bed; zip tied the boy's wrists and ankles and applied tape over the young man's mouth. He then pulled the boy over his shoulder and carried him downstairs.

The other two men moved to the kitchen and disconnected the gas line under the Thermador cooktop. One of the men set a small disposable incendiary device next the gas line after adjusting the timer for four minutes.

Joseph Wu was bundled into the back of the Explorer. They were two blocks away when the explosion obliterated the Wu home.

An hour later they turned onto a small country road, driving until they found an abandoned field. They pulled the boy from the back of the SUV and carried him into the field. One man killed the young man while the other two dug his grave. They had been instructed to remove the young man from his home, so that it would appear that he had not been home when it was destroyed. The authorities learned later that Joseph Wu had been visiting and staying the night at his beloved aunt and uncles' home in nearby Frisco Texas.

CHAPTER 2

Jonathan Scanlan had finished browsing through the San Francisco Chronicle, took a last sip from his coffee mug, and glanced across the room at his Labrador. Bo was playing with one of his toys, a rubber pig that squeaked when squeezed. Jonathan was debating taking Bo for a run in the Presidio or hitting some golf balls at the Harding Park driving range, when his cell phone chirped. He was surprised to see Cal Hulse's name on the screen.

"Cal, I can't believe you're up this early."

"I know. I had to be on an early telephone conference with some people at INA. How about dinner tonight?"

"Sure, any place in mind?"

"No, you pick. Call me when it's lined up and leave a message. I'm going back to bed."

It was too early to make reservations, so Jonathan decided a run in the Presidio was called for. When he mentioned the word run to Bo, the Lab dropped his toy and began jumping around the room.

Later, Jonathan made reservations and called Cal, leaving a voicemail message. "Seven at Harris. I'll line up an Uber ride and pick you up at six forty."

Jonathan and Cal met when they were attending the University of California at Berkeley. Both were on scholarships; Jonathan, on an athletic scholarship with the golf team, while Cal had a full-ride academic scholarship. They became best friends with a bond that only grew stronger over time.

In many ways, the two men were a study in contrasts. Jonathan was tall and had retained his athletic build, while Cal was of medium height and could politely be described as hefty. Cal was an avid sports fan, following all the Bay Area's professional teams as well as those at Cal. His interest in sports was as a fan, never as a participant. In high school, Jonathan had been a star player on the baseball team and on the golf course. The University of California athletic director wanted Jonathan to be on the school's baseball team, but he decided to focus his talents on golf. He quickly became the team's top player.

Cal attended the tournaments whenever he could, which was how and where the two young men met.

After college, Cal became the most sought-after high-tech consultant west of the Mississippi. When Jonathan graduated, he tried to qualify as a touring golf pro, but could not make the cut. He returned to Berkeley for a master's and PHD in literature. After a stint teaching contemporary American literature at San Francisco State, he left teaching and became a bestselling nonfiction author. As a result of two lawsuits, and his writing skills, Jonathan joined the one percent.

———

Once Cal and Jonathan were settled in at their table at the Van Ness steakhouse, Jonathan ordered a glass of Chardonnay while Cal opted for a Gimlet. Cal smiled at Jonathan's choice. "Chardonnay? What happened to my beer buddy?"

Jonathan had to smile. "I still like my beer, but Cory has steered me into enjoying wine. By the way, you need to come over to the house. She helped me upgrade the furnishings."

"So, everything is going well with you and Cory?"

"Could not be better."

"Any chance she might be moving in?"

Jonathan shook his head. "No. We haven't had that conversation.

Besides, with her being back at Lockheed, the commute from the city to Sunnyvale would be a problem."

Cal knew Jonathan was not big on discussing his personal relationships and changed the subject. "Have you started writing about Independence?"

"Yes, and it's going well. I think I can wrap it up fairly soon."

The investigation of a defense contractor named Independence had put Jonathan, Cal, and Cory Bishop's lives at risk. Several people had died violently in a deadly cat and mouse race to uncover the company's secrets.

Both men had ordered steaks and were sharing a Pine Ridge Cabernet. The conversation stalled as they focused on their dinners. At one point, Jonathan looked up at his friend. "What about you? Have you been busy?"

Cal shook his head. "No, it's been fairly slow which is fine with me after our Independence adventure. Have you heard how Myron is doing?"

"He's still in physical therapy, but it's going well." Jonathan had brought in Myron Rossi to protect him and his friends during the Independence investigation. Myron had been shot during the final confrontation.

As they shared the last of the cab, the conversation shifted to the San Francisco 49ers and whether the rookies could fill the void left by the departed veterans.

When Jonathan returned home, his thoughts went back to Cal's questions about his relationship with Cory. Cory had joined Jonathan and Cal as they investigated possible fraud and abuse among defense contractors. Their investigation led them down a dangerous path when they focused on one highly secretive contractor.

Jonathan and Cory's relationship became serious as they attempted to survive and uncover the secrets the contractor was hiding. In the aftermath of their adventures, they had settled into a comfortable pattern, together on weekends, but living separately. Jonathan had no idea if Cory wanted to move to the next step, and was ambivalent about it himself, but he could not Invision not having Cory in his life

CHAPTER 3

Two days later, Cal was in his condominium paying bills when his phone rang. As usual, he let it go to voicemail. Later, when he was checking his messages, he listened to one from an unfamiliar number.

"Mr. Hulse, my name is Forrest Woodward, and I'm with the Defense Intelligence Agency. I'd like to talk to you about a project. Please call me at 202 555-1627."

Cal considered not returning the man's call, but curiosity prevailed.

"Mr. Woodward, this is Cal Hulse returning your call."

"Thank you. Would it be possible for us to meet?"

Cal had no interest in flying to DC. "Where are you?"

"I'm in San Francisco."

Cal glanced at his watch. "I can meet with you this afternoon at 3:00."

"Great, I'll come to your place."

"You know where I live?"

The man laughed. "We are an intelligence agency."

At exactly 3:00, the doorbell rang and Cal buzzed Woodward into the building. Cal opened the door to his unit and stepped outside to greet his visitor. The man who stepped out of the elevator was quite tall, midthirties and appeared to be in excellent shape. He was clean shaven, had close-cut brown hair, somewhat sharp facial features and, Cal thought, a military bearing.

The man smiled as he approached Cal, extended his hand and said, "Forrest Woodward."

Cal shook Woodward's hand and led him into his condo. Woodward stopped and gazed around the room at Cal's sports collectibles. "Wow, quite a collection."

Cal gave a small smile. "Mostly from the local teams."

"I live in DC, but still follow my Chicago teams."

Cal motioned Woodward into his living room. "Can I get you anything, water or coffee?"

"No thanks, I'm good." Woodward took a seat on the sofa and Cal joined him on a facing chair.

"Can you tell me about the project you mentioned?"

"It's classified so until a confidentiality agreement is signed, I can only speak in general terms. Basically, information is being leaked to one of our country's adversaries and we would like you to help us find the leaker."

Cal sat back and thought about the potential project. After a moment he said, "Why come to me? Surly you have enormous resources to bring to bear on the problem."

"We do. Your investigation would run parallel to the one at the DIA." Woodward smiled and added, "We're coming to you because we understand you're the best."

"I'm flattered, but again, the government has a great deal of resources that I don't have."

"We're aware of how you figured out what was happening at Independence."

"That was a team effort."

"No. You figured it out. Your friends just kept you alive."

Cal took a moment to consider the project. He had never worked directly for the government but, when he thought about it, the only real difference from his regular clients would be who would be writing the checks.

"All right, I'm not sure if I can solve your problem, but I'm willing to try."

Woodward smiled and pulled several forms from his briefcase. "If you'll complete these forms, I'll be able to give you more detailed information."

Cal moved to his kitchen table and began completing the paperwork. When he was finished, he handed the completed forms to Woodward, "I'll like to receive copies."

"Of course. The information being leaked relates to our defense plans for Taiwan. The Chinese have taken countermeasures to block some of our planned efforts. We believe the leak is coming from the DOD, although it's possible it could be coming from State or the White House."

"When will you be providing me with the information you have?"

"In the next day or two. We'll also be setting you up with one of our computers and secure encrypted communication gear."

Forrest Woodward shook Cal's hand and was out the door.

CHAPTER 4

Jonathan sat back at his desk and stared at his computer. He had just finished the last page of his new book. He picked up his phone and called his literary agent. She answered on the first ring.

"Mary Downs Literary Agency."

"Mary, its Jonathan. I just finished my next book."

"That's great, Jonathan. What's it about?"

"We uncovered an unbelievable situation at a major defense contractor named Independence."

"I never heard of the company."

"Trust me, this is a really big story. I'm sending the manuscript off to my editor for a cleanup. I expect she'll take about two weeks."

"Okay. What's the title?"

"*The Independence Conspiracy*. I think you'll like it."

"I'm sure I will."

Jonathan called Cory. "Hey, I just finished the book on Independence. Let's celebrate and get away for the weekend."

"I'm all in. What are you thinking?"

"Carmel. I did a little research. Are you all right if we bring Bo?"

"Sure. Are there dog-friendly places in Carmel?"

"Several. I'll make a reservation. Pick you up Saturday, about ten?"

"I'll be ready."

Jonathan turned to Bo. "We're going on a little trip." Bo seemed happy but did not reply.

Saturday morning, Jonathan bundled his bag and Bo into his Jeep, along with Bo's dog bed and provisions. Jonathan had recovered his well-used Jeep from the San Carlos impound yard after the dust settled on the Independence affair.

The weather was clear and crisp as Jonathan drove down to Cory's condominium in San Carlos. Jonathan never ceased to be amazed that this gorgeous, incredibly intelligent woman was now part of his life. She was waiting and stepped out of her building as Jonathan pulled in front. She laughed as she received kisses from both Jonathan and Bo. There was little traffic, and they made the drive in under two hours. It was too early to check into their room at the Cypress Inn, so they dropped off their bags, parked in the lot, and walked with Bo over to Ocean Avenue.

The threesome leisurely walked past the boutiques and galleries, finally stopping at a café with outdoor seating. Jonthan and Cory ordered coffee and pastries while Bo was given a bowl of water.

When they returned to the Inn, they went to their room and unpacked. With several hours before their dinner reservation at Anton & Michel, they took Bo to the nearby beach. He was able to mingle with several other dogs, but they kept him out of the water. A soaking wet Lab would not be welcome at the Cypress Inn.

Bo stayed in the room when they went to dinner. They shared a red and golden beet salad and a bottle of Chardonnay. Jonathan ordered the rack of lamb, while Cory went with salmon. Neither had room for dessert. During dinner, Cory brought Jonathan up to speed on the gossip at Lockheed, and Jonathan told her about his conversation with Mary Downs.

Later, Bo was banished to his dog bed in the living room while Jonathan and Cory took full advantage of the queen-sized bed.

After a late breakfast, they took Bo for another walk around the charming town before heading back home.

A week later, Jonathan and Bo had just returned from a morning run when his cell chirped. He saw from the screen it was coming from Mary Downs.

"Morning, Mary. I guess for you it should be good afternoon."

"Hi, Jonathan. I received *The Independence Conspiracy* and loved it. Did people really chase you, Cory Bishop, and Cal Hulse, all over the Bay Area, trying to kill you?"

"All true. They were mainly after Cal. Cory and I were collateral damage."

"And Independence was owned by the Chinese government?"

"That was the big secret."

"Unbelievable. I'll start shopping it around. I believe the publishing houses will compete for this one."

"Sounds great, Mary. Keep me posted."

CHAPTER 5

Joseph Wu sat in his cubicle at the Pentagon, working on a briefing report. General Michael Kelly stopped and patted the young man on his back.

"I was sorry to see that Ohio State beat your Longhorns."

Joseph looked up, smiled, and said in his broad Texas accent, "Maybe next year."

"How's the report going?"

"I'll have it finished by the end of the day."

"Great work." The general again patted the man's back before strolling back to his office.

The general's briefing notes contained little of real interest, but Wu nevertheless transferred the information to a thumb drive. Later that evening he walked into Meridian Hill Park, sat briefly on one of the park benches, and taped the device to the bottom of the bench. He then continued his walk through the park and on to his apartment.

Wu, whose birth name was actually Yuze Zhao, held no political beliefs, nor was he a member of the Communist Party. He simply was doing what he had been trained to do. He had been born in a small village on the outskirts of Chengdu, in the central Sichuan Province.

His intellectual abilities were apparent at a very young age. A talent spotter from the CCP heard about the gifted boy and arranged a series of tests. Yuze Zhao's scores were literally off the charts.

The boy was then separated from his parents and placed in a program for intellectually gifted young boys and girls. Here he received his new name, Joseph Wu. After three years, Wu was transferred to a new facility which closely resembled an American community. Only American food was served, which took some getting used to, and only English was spoken. Only American television shows were available and only Western clothing could be worn.

The academic curriculum was challenging, but easily absorbed by Wu. An understanding of American sports was required. While Wu had no problem figuring out football, baseball and basketball, when asked to participate, it became quickly apparent that the young man was not an athlete.

At one point in his training, Wu was instructed to learn to speak with a broad Texas accent. This he did find to be difficult. It took over a year of listening to tapes and practice before he could speak like Willie Nelson.

Just shy of his nineteenth birthday, Wu was smuggled into Taiwan. Armed with forged documents, Wu was guided to the Taoyuan International Airport and placed on a plane bound for Los Angeles.

After clearing customs, Wu was greeted by a middle-aged man named Allen Chen. Chen took Wu to a hotel near the airport to decompress after his long journey. Two days later, Chen and Wu embarked on a cross-country road trip to the town of Frisco, just outside Dallas.

They finally arrived at the modest home of Harriet and Jason Liu. Wu had been instructed to refer to the couple as his aunt and uncle. His legend was that he came to live with the Lius after his parents had been killed in a natural gas explosion at their home. His new aunt and uncle did not appear to be overjoyed to receive their new nephew into their home.

Chen had provided Wu with papers showing his school records from Marcus High School in Flower Mound. He would be attending Memorial High School in Frisco for his senior year. As Wu glanced at his new home and his new relatives, he was pleased that his stay in Frisco would be brief.

Wu went to the room that was to be his bedroom. When he came back, he told Chen that he would need a computer and a printer. Chen nodded and said he would deliver them the next day. Chen explained the process that had been done to enroll the young man in the high school.

Wu breezed through his senior year at Memorial, achieving straight As, and was accepted at the University of Texas at Austin. He lived in a dorm on campus and actually enjoyed his college experience. He remained aloof from the other students and made no close friends.

He graduated in three years and, when offered to be the class valedictorian, he politely refused. Wu participated in on-campus interviews and, as a result, received several offers. He accepted an offer of an entry-level position at the State Department.

Chen had leased a modest apartment in Wu's name in DC. The young man found his duties at the State to be trivial and boring, but he applied himself and, over time, his brilliant mind was noticed. He quickly rose in the bureaucracy and became known as a young man going places. When an opening occurred at the Pentagon, Wu jumped on it. Two years later, he was General Michael Kelly's most trusted aide.

CHAPTER 6

Jonathan's morning routine was interrupted by a call. A glance at the screen showed it was Mary Downs.

"Good morning, Jonathan."

"Morning, Mary, how are you?"

"I'm fine, and as I told you earlier, I loved the book. I shopped it around, and unlike *The Culprit Murders*, everybody was excited. We have offers from most of the big names. The best deal is from Macmillan. Two hundred thousand up front and a very healthy amount for promotion."

"That's great, Mary. Will I have to go on a book signing tour?"

"No. They do want you to do a couple of interviews."

"I'm fine with that."

"I'll send you a copy of the contract."

After the call, Jonathan sat back and thought about the difference between the Macmillan offer and the industry's lukewarm reaction to *Culprits of the American Culture* and *The Culprit Murders*. Not long ago, he would have been celebrating Macmillan's offer. While he was happy with the offer, the money now had little impact on his life, but he did want to share the news with Cal and Cory.

As usual, his call to Cal went to voicemail.

Later in the morning, Cal returned the call. "Hi Jon, what's up?"

"I just got a great offer for my book from Macmillan. My treat for dinner."

"Sure, I could use a break. Where do you want to go?"

"How about Boulevard? I'll make a reservation and pick you up with Uber. See you at seven."

"You're on."

On the ride down to Boulevard, Jonathan noticed Cal's somber expression. When they were seated with drinks in hand, he turned to his friend. "You seem a little off tonight."

"I'm working on a new project, and it's not going very well."

"Can you tell me about it?"

Cal shook his head. "I'd like to, but I can't."

"Well, I'm sure you'll figure it out."

"I'm not sure I can."

Jonathan stared at his friend. Cal's pessimistic attitude was not the norm. "Is it with INA?"

"No, I can't go into the details, but it's with the government."

"Wow, the government. If I remember right, they haven't been your friend."

Cal forced a smile. "I know, but this is with a different area of the government. I see the Warriors have resigned Payton."

As they worked through their dinner, the conversation turned to the 49ers losing Bosa for the season and the team's special team problems.

The following day, Cal contacted Forrest Woodward. Woodward's first words were, "Any progress?"

"That's what I'm calling you about. The information you provided is great, but it only describes the problem. I believe we need to look at all the people who had access to the DOD plans."

"We have people doing that."

"With what success?"

There was a long pause. "Not much so far."

"I'd like to bring in the team that worked on Independence, Jonathan Scanlan and Cory Bishop." Cal knew better than to mention Myron Rossi.

"I don't see how I can do that."

"Well, stop paying me because this is going nowhere."

"A week later, Woodward called. "I got an okay for Cory Bishop because of her security clearance at Lockheed, but it's a no-go on Scanlan."

"Cory isn't going to agree to work with us without Jonathan." With that statement, Cal hung up on the Defense Intelligence Agency agent.

Two weeks later, Woodward called. "All right, Scanlan is in. He'll have to sign a dozen forms, and I'll need to meet with both of them before they're given any information."

"First, let me see if they're willing to sign up."

"Call me when you have their answer."

Cal immediately called Jonathan. "Jon, I received a tentative green light to include you and Cory on the project I couldn't talk about at dinner. Get ahold of Cory and let's meet at my place."

Friday after work, Cory drove up to Jonathan's home in the city. After dropping off her bag they took an Uber to Cal's condo in Pacific Heights.

Once settled in his living room, Cal described, in general terms, that sensitive information was being leaked to a foreign government and that he had been tasked with identifying the leaker.

Both Jonathan and Cory sat in silence for a moment, absorbing what Cal had related. Finally, Cory spoke. "I'm not willing to leave my job at Lockheed."

Cal nodded. "I understand. What about you, Jon?"

"I'll work with you. If this involves a lot of travel, I'll have to figure out what to do with Bo. I don't want to shove him in a kennel for an extended period of time."

"Okay. The next step is a meeting with my contact, an agent with the Defense Intelligence Agency named Forrest Woodward."

When Jonathan and Cory left, Cal called Woodward, knowing it would be eleven o'clock in DC.

He was surprised when the man answered immediately. "All right, I met with Jonathan and Cory. Jonathan was agreeable, but Cory said she wasn't willing to leave her job at Lockheed."

"I think I can make that work for Bishop. You didn't give them any details."

"No more than you gave me before I signed up."

"Okay, I'll be flying out in the next day or two. I'll let you know."

Woodward called the following morning and left a message. "I'll be in San Francisco by six this evening. Please have Bishop and Scanlan at your place by seven thirty."

When the agent arrived at Cal's condominium, he found the three friends arrayed around Cal's living room. He entered the room and, Jonathan thought, offered a politician's smile.

Woodward remained standing as he motioned Jonathan, Cal, and Cory back to their seats. "All right. If you agree to take part in this investigation, you have to agree not to disclose any of the information I will be sharing with you." Jonathan noticed that the agent seemed highly focused on Cory. As a stunningly beautiful, tall blonde woman with a show-stopping figure, the attention was understandable. While understandable, Jonathan was becoming increasingly pissed.

Cory stood up. "I'm sure Cal told you that I'm not willing to leave my job at Lockheed to work on this investigation."

"We have discussed this situation with senior management at Lockheed, and they have agreed to place you on an extended leave. You could return to your job when the investigation is over."

Jonathan spoke up. "As you're aware, I'm an author of nonfiction books. If there is a story at the end of this, I would want to write about it. I would agree to not disclose anything that would jeopardize our country."

Woodward shook his head. "That is unacceptable. If you're out, Hulse can continue his end of the investigation, and Cory and I will do the field work."

Jonathan stood up and said, "Then I'm out of here."

Cory said, "Then I'm also out."

Cory joined Jonathan as he crossed the room toward the door. The agent watched as the plan he had pushed through his agency was coming apart. "Wait, be reasonable. This information is classified."

Jonathan stopped and turned back to Woodward. "Everything Independence was doing was classified."

"But this is different." The agent was sputtering. Jonathan noticed that the polished, James Bond persona had evaporated.

"If you want me involved, I won't be signing any of your forms."

Forrest Woodward's mind was racing. He had invested career capital in involving Cal Hulse, and later Scanlan and Bishop. He visualized a transfer from DC to Des Moines.

In desperation, the agent almost shouted. "What if you're off the books?"

"That would be fine. I wasn't going to ask to be paid. Cory will need to be paid, as I doubt Lockheed would keep her on salary while she's working for you."

"We can do that."

There was an uncomfortable silence as Jonathan and Cory returned to their seats. A still slightly rattled Agent Woodward provided Jonathan and Cory with the same briefing he had earlier given to Cal. Neither asked any questions until he was finished.

Jonathan turned to Cal. "Have you received a list of everyone who was briefed on the plans for Taiwan?"

Cal nodded. "The detailed plans were kept on a need-to-know basis. At this time, I'd say, about forty people, mostly at DOD, and of course, that includes a few people at the White House."

Jonathan looked at his watch. "All right. It's getting late. Let's meet tomorrow and figure out where we go from here."

Woodward glanced around the room. "Shouldn't we start right now? I have a lot of ideas."

Jonathan offered a thin smile. "I'm sure you do. We'll keep you informed."

As Jonathan drove Cory back to his new home, she turned to him and asked, "You obviously didn't want to hear the man's ideas. Why not?"

"He's a career bureaucrat. His ideas are what his agency is currently doing, without success, or we wouldn't have been brought in."

"You don't trust him?"

"I'm sure he's honest, but like I said, he's a bureaucrat. I believe he'd throw up more barriers than provide real help." Jonathan was also not pleased with the agent's interest in Cory.

Cory thought about it and finally nodded in agreement.

CHAPTER 7

After Jonathan and Cory had a light breakfast, Jonathan called Cal. As usual, it went to voicemail. Cal was definitely not a morning person. "Cal, we'll be at your place about ten."

Jonathan took Bo for a walk around the neighborhood, and later, he and Cory shared their ideas about how to approach the investigation. One of Jonathan's concerns was having to leave Bo if a good deal of travel was involved. He did not want to put his adopted child in a kennel.

Normally, street parking near Cal's condo was problematic, but Jonathan was lucky and found a space a half block away. When they reached Cal's unit, he offered coffee as they took seats around his breakfast table.

Jonathan looked at Cal. "You said about forty people knew about the plans for Taiwan. We need to narrow the list."

Cory gave him a questioning glance. "How can we do that?"

Jonathan thought for a minute. "Having access to the plans isn't the same as seeing the plans or being briefed. Access means people who have positions that would allow them access. Some of those people could have been unavailable, like on leave or on assignment out of the country."

Cal nodded. "I can have Woodward check that out."

"Let's focus initially on DOD personnel. Conventional wisdom seems to believe the leaks are coming from there. If we come up dry, we can take a look at the White House and people at State."

Cory had a thought. "Why would someone in a responsible government job betray his or her country?"

Cal said, "Money, or some major grievance."

Jonathan nodded. "We can't ignore the possibility that it's a mole, a Manchurian Candidate kind of thing."

The three sat back and thought about that possibility. Cal said, "That's a scary thought."

"But one we have to consider."

Jonathan patted Cal on his shoulder. "Give Woodward a call. Let's get together when we have the pared-down list."

Cory turned to Cal and Jonathan. "You know, I'm only in this if Lockheed puts me on leave."

Cal nodded, "Woodward told me that senior management at Lockheed has agreed. The government has a lot of influence when it comes to defense contractors."

As they walked back to Jonathan's Jeep, he turned to Cory, "We can't really do anything until we get the new list. Why don't we take Bo and go to lunch in Marin? I know Perry's in Larkspur is dog-friendly."

"That sounds like fun."

As soon as Jonathan and Cory left, Cal called Forrest Woodward. "Forrest, this is Cal. We need your people to find out who on the list you provided was not available when the defense plans were distributed."

"What do you mean, not available?"

"On leave, out of the country on assignment. Basically, not briefed."

It took a moment for the wheels to turn. "I see where you're going. Okay, but it'll take a little time."

When he was off the phone, Cal picked up the list. There were forty-two names on the list. Four were at the White House, and three were at State. So, if they focused on the DOD, they were down to thirty-five.

CHAPTER 8

Over the last year, China has become increasingly belligerent and threatening toward Taiwan. An array of battle ships cruised the Taiwan Strait, and Chinese Sukhoi Au 27s fighter jets intentionally invaded Taiwan's airspace. Occasionally, China used its Lockheed Martin F-22 Raptors on those invasive flights, basically giving the finger to American leadership.

China's clear provocations created increasing pressure on the American president to define his country's posture should China attack the island nation. While America had always supported Taiwan, the country's position on Taiwan had always been somewhat vague.

The critical question was, would the United States go to war with China to defend Taiwan? The position papers that Joseph Wu had passed on to his handler presented arguments for and against such action. The communications received by Allen Chen were more and more strident in their demands to know the answer.

Chen knew Wu could not provide evidence of a clear decision from General Kelly's office, a fact that his masters in Beijing did not seem to understand. Listening to the commentators at CNN and Fox was equally unhelpful.

In frustration, Chen wanted to tell Beijing to just make a wild assed guess, but he knew that doing so would limit his future.

———

While the Pentagon was not willing to provide copies of the briefings that had obviously influenced Chinese military behavior, they did list six people who had not been privy to all those documents.

As Jonathan, Cory, and Cal huddled in Cal's condominium, they studied the remaining list of twenty-nine people. Cal looked at his friends. "That's still a lot of potential leakers."

Jonathan nodded. "Well, it's a start. Let's try to think of ways to eliminate as many as possible."

Cory sat back, her eyes distant in thought. "When we considered why someone would betray their country, we said, money and ideological beliefs."

Cal nodded. "Hates his or her country."

"Right. So, can we eliminate people who don't have money problems and don't hate their country?"

Cal said, "I can figure out the money part, but how do we know if a person hates our country. If they work for the Department of Defense, they probably don't go to peace rallies."

Jonathan thought for a moment. "If it's not money, it would have to be someone who believes the Beijing line, that Taiwan should be part of China."

Cal looked dubious. "How can we know what someone is thinking?"

Cory said, "What about the tariffs we imposed on China. Wouldn't they think it's something we shouldn't be doing?"

Cal, ever the critic, said, "I doubt tariffs would be a big enough deal to betray your country."

Jonathan had a thought. "They might express their opinions to their family or friends, even coworkers, or on social media."

Cal shrugged. "Maybe."

"We need to know more about these people besides name, rank, and serial number."

Cory sat up. "What about donations? Would a traitor donate money to something like Tunnels to Towers?"

Cal considered Cory's comment. "No, he wouldn't. No one but your tax guy would have that type of information. The leaker would be more likely to donate to Code Pink."

Jonathan stared at his friend. "How would we know about someone's donations?"

"I don't think you really want to know the details, but virtually all tax filings go through the internet. It'll take some digging, but I can get the information. Remember, unless we can eliminate more people, there are twenty-nine on the list. It's going to take some time."

Jonathan nodded. "Okay. Is everything we're doing getting to Woodward?"

Cal shook his head. "This is the first time I've had anything to give him."

"Why don't you keep it a little vague?" This brought a puzzled expression from Cal.

"I think if he sees progress, he's going to want to jump in and micromanage us."

"Really?'

"We can't cut him out because we need him to keep feeding us information, but if he sees we're making progress, he'll want to run the show, and I don't think that would work out well."

After a moment's hesitation, Cal nodded. "I have the impression he believes he's always the smartest man in the room."

CHAPTER 9

Agent Woodward was receiving increasing pressure from his superiors. He wanted to point out that his Defense Intelligence Agency and several other agencies at the DOD had been exerting mammoth manpower for almost two months without any positive results, but he knew such a comment would not be well received.

While understanding the unfairness of the situation, he decided he had to turn that pressure on to Cal Hulse. He demanded daily updates and became abusive when he was told that the process would take time. At one point, Cal told the agent that he would call when he had something to report. After that conversation, Cal stopped answering Woodward's calls.

Two weeks had passed when Cal called Jonathan. "Let's get together."

Jonathan could hear the urgency in Cal's voice. "Sure, can you tell me what you have?"

"Not over the phone. Let me know when Cory can join us. We'll meet at your place."

When Jonathan called Cory, she simply said, "Give me two hours."

Cory arrived before Cal. "Any idea what he has?"

"None, but from his voice, it sounded positive."

A highly animated Cal arrived minutes later. He motioned toward the living room, and Jonathan and Cory followed. Both were tense as they sat on the edge of their chairs.

Cal looked at his friends. "We don't have the leaker, but we have narrowed the list." He turned to Cory. "Your idea really worked. I guess folks in the military disproportionally support specific types of charities."

He pulled out a list. "The major ones are Tunnels to Towers, the Wounded Warrior Project, and Disabled American Veterans. But there were quite a few more, K9s For Warriors, Operation Homefront, and the Semper Fi Fund, for example."

Jonathan was clearly growing impatient. "So, how many on the list donated to these organizations?"

"Twenty of the remaining twenty-nine."

"Leaving at nine."

Cal smiled and nodded. "Of course, it isn't a foolproof indicator, but why would a traitor make a donation to these charities?"

Cory leaned back. "So, what do we do now?"

Cal smiled and said with enthusiasm, "We do a deep dive into the remaining nine."

Jonathan laughed, "You mean, you do a deep dive?"

"Well, yes."

Cory leaned forward. "I spent some time over the last two weeks studying the characteristics of known traitors, looking for common traits. You know, single or married, gregarious or loner, things like that."

Neither Jonathan nor Cal spoke as they waited for her findings. "Almost all were single. Most were loners, but there were exceptions."

Jonathan was impressed with the woman's creative thinking. "When we look at the nine, we can keep those traits in mind."

When their meeting broke up, and Cal returned to his condo, there was another phone message from Forrest Woodward. The agent was no longer pleasant or polite. "If I don't receive a status report within the next twenty-four hours, we will consider you in violation of your contract and no longer a consultant to our agency."

Cal was not bothered by the tone or the message. After years of dealing with the dictatorial behavior of a number of high-tech executives, he was used to this type of attitude. The message did prompt him to consider whether he wanted to continue to work with the man. He knew Jonathan and Cory would want to continue the investigation, with or without the agent's involvement. After several moments of internal debate, Cal decided there was an advantage to keep using Woodward as an information resource.

He sat down at the agency's computer and composed an email.

We have narrowed the list of potential leakers down to nine individuals: William Barron, Raymond Handy, James Farrell, Susan Giambruno, Robert Nunemann, Thomas Doherty, William Hamlin, Seth Cannon and Michael Kelly

Please provide all, and I mean all, professional and personal information you have on these individuals.

Even though it was quite late in DC, Woodward's reply was almost immediate.

How did you reduce the list to these nine names?

Cal had no interest in explaining the process.

They met our criteria. Just provide the information.

Three days later, voluminous files were sent electronically to Cal's agency server. Cal immediately called Jonathan. "We have a ton of information on the nine. I'm going to need help wading through it."

"I'll call Cory. She's at her place in San Carlos. Print everything out. We'll start reviewing the stuff tomorrow."

They met at Cal's condominium the following day and agreed to divide the files, each receiving three sets of information. They agreed to make notes when coming across anything of interest. Reviewing the information was a painfully slow process; at the end of the day, each member of the team had only completed the review of one of the eight men and one woman.

At the end of the third day, they pushed aside the last of the files and reviewed their notes.

Jonathan looked over at Cory. "Anything stand out?"

"No, not really. Colonel Susan Giambruno grew up in a military family. Moved up quickly through the ranks, particularly for a woman. Nothing interesting. Colonel Robert Nunemann pretty much said the same thing. Not from a military family, but saw combat in Afghanistan. General William Hamlin, like the others, was a West Point graduate with an unblemished career.

"Cal?"

"Nothing on Barron or Handy. General Seth Cannon recently purchased a very expensive new home. Generals make good money, but not enough to afford something in this price range. How about you?"

Jonathan said, "I didn't see anything questionable on Farrell or Kelly. General Kelly held posts in South Korea and the Philippines before his position at the Pentagon, but that's probably not important. Colonel Thomas Doherty is heavily in debt. A combination of a divorce and some bad investments."

Cal stood up and poured himself another cup of coffee. "Okay, for starters, let's take a closer look at Colonel Doherty and General Cannon. We're getting close to the point where you will have to spend time in DC, taking an up close and personal look at the nine possibilities."

As if reading Jonathan's mind, Cory said, "Maybe your parents could take care of Bo."

Jonathan nodded. "I've thought about that. Problem is, they've never had a pet, but I'm going to give them a call."

CHAPTER 10

The following morning, Jonathan picked up his phone and dialed his parents' number. He knew his parents were kind, loving people, but he was not optimistic about their willingness to take care of Bo. If they loved dogs, why had they never had one?

When Thomas answered, Jonathan smiled. "Hi, Dad, how is everything going?"

"Everything's fine, Jon. How about you? We read your new book. You never mentioned how much danger you were in."

"It all worked out. I have a favor to ask. You know I have a Labrador named Bo. I'm going to have to travel fairly soon. Could you and Mom take care of him when I'm gone? He's really well behaved."

There was a long pause. "I don't know. We've never had a pet. How long will you be gone?"

"I'm not sure, maybe a couple of weeks."

"I'd have to talk to your mother. By the way, when are we going to meet Cory?"

"Soon, Dad. I'm sure you'll like her."

"I'm sure we will. By the way, you need to stop sending us money. We really don't need it."

"Dad, I've told you. I have more money than I'll ever need. Better you than the tax man."

"Well, I'll call you after I talk to your mom."

"Thanks, Dad."

Jonathan was worried that his parents would be unwilling to take in Bo. It was one thing to have him spend a night at the local doggie spa; it was another to have him kenneled for weeks. He decided to withdraw from the investigation if Bo was not going to St. George.

Later that evening, when his phone rang, he saw that it was his parents. He answered, anticipating the worst.

"Evening, Jon. Your mom and I talked it over, and we're willing to take care of Bo."

Jonathan let out a sigh of relief. "I really appreciate it, Dad. Like I said, he's really a great dog. I'll let you know when I'll be bringing him."

"We look forward to seeing you, and I guess Bo."

One week later, Jonathan and Bo were on the road. Unfortunately, the trip was long and boring. When they reached Bakersfield and turned east toward Las Vegas, Jonathan turned off the highway for gas and a pit stop. After Jonathan and Bo had relieved themselves, they continued across California as the Jeep's radio continued to blast out 60's rock. After eleven hours, the weary road warriors arrived at St. George, Utah.

Thomas and Linda Scanlan stepped out of their modest home to greet their son and Bo. Hugs were shared as they led Jonathan and Bo into their one-story rancher. After Bo's food, bed, and toys were brought into the house, Jonathan relaxed in the living room with a beer as Bo lapped up water from his bowl.

His father smiled at his son. "We're so proud of you. A bestselling author, it's unbelievable."

His mother leaned forward in her chair. "You have to tell us all about Cory. Are you two getting serious?"

"Mom, come on. Yes, we're together, but we'll see where it goes."

Thomas chimed in. "I went to her Facebook page. She's an absolute knockout."

Jonathan, who had not known Cory had a Facebook page, simply smiled. Knowing his mother would keep pressing him about Cory,

Jonathan changed the subject. "You guys have to come out to San Francisco and see my new home."

"We went on Google and checked it out. It's beautiful. What made you make the move from your old apartment? You were there forever."

"I just decided I was ready for a change. With money from the books and the lawsuits against San Francisco State and the FBI, I could afford the change. Besides, I wanted a dog, and that wouldn't work at the apartment." Bo sat by Jonathan's side.

His father looked at Bo. "He seems devoted to you. Do you think he'll be okay when you leave?"

"He'll adjust. Just give him a lot of treats and attention."

Jonathan sensed that his mother was more concerned about Bo than his father. "I know you've never had pets, but just treat Bo like one of the family."

"When do you have to go back?"

"The day after tomorrow. If it's all right with you, I'd like to leave the Jeep here and fly back."

Thomas said, "Sure. You said you'd be traveling. Can you tell us where?"

"I'll be going to the Washington DC area. I can't tell you more; it involves the government."

Linda looked concerned. "Will it be dangerous?"

"No, not at all."

Both parents had read Jonathan's books and provided skeptical expressions, but did not press the issue.

His father's expression showed his concern. "Have you heard from Rick?"

Rick Scanlan was Jonathan's younger brother. While only a year apart in age, they had never been close. In high school, Jonathan had been focused on sports and academics, while Rick had focused on partying and hanging out with friends who were equally unmotivated. When Jonathan moved on to college, Rick dropped out of school and began running into problems with the legal system. When Jonathan discovered that Rick had taken money out of his parents' retirement accounts, their confrontation became violent.

After years of avoiding each other, Rick had approached his brother and asked for money to bail himself out of a financial bind. Jonathan had refused. Jonathan did not see the point in telling his parents about Rick's latest financial problems.

The only positive thing to come out of Rick's situation was Myron Rossi. Myron had been sent by a loan shark to have Jonathan cover Rick's debt. Jonathan had again refused, but, later, Myron became Jonathan's protector and friend.

"No, Dad. I haven't heard from Rick for quite a while."

His mother stood up. "Well, you must be famished. I made a pot roast Come on, let's have dinner."

CHAPTER 11

Jonahan's flight back to San Francisco was quick and uneventful. As soon as he arrived home, he began packing for the next day's trip to the nation's capital. He thought back to the flight he and Cory had taken earlier and Cory's white-knuckle fear of flying. He had offered to make train reservations for this trip, but Cory had assured him that her supply of Zoloft would take care of the problem. He hoped she was right.

When they reached the airport, Cory was not showing the tension that had earlier consumed her. She popped her pills as they waited to board. Knowing she would probably sleep during the flight, she handed Jonathan a thick manila envelope.

"Here are the bios on each of the nine. If Zoloft works like the stuff I took before, I'll become really sleepy. You can use the time to study what we put together."

Jonathan smiled. "Okay. How are you feeling?"

She squeezed his arm. "I'll be fine."

Jonathan had booked first-class reservations, and once on board and in the air, Cory reclined her seat and was soon asleep. Jonathan lowered his tray and began reviewing the information. After three hours, he slid the reports back into the envelope and sat back. Nothing had really jumped out.

Jonathan gently shook Cory awake as they began their descent into the Ronald Reagan Airport. She was still groggy as they made their way off the plane and eventually to the cab stand. A short ride later, they pulled in front of the Ritz-Carlton hotel in Pentagon City.

After checking in, Jonathan helped Cory to their room and, shortly later, into bed. Hunger pangs drove Jonathan to the hotel's main restaurant, where he ordered a ribeye and a Ceaser salad. Later, in their room, he watched a movie on Turner Classics with the volume turned down.

He woke to the sound of running water and realized Cory was no longer in bed. When he looked out the bedroom window, he saw the faint light of early dawn. He made a low moaning sound as he lay back under the covers. Moments later, Cory stepped out of the bathroom.

"Sorry to wake you. I just couldn't sleep anymore. Go back to sleep, I'm going to go for a walk around the hotel grounds."

"Be careful, DC isn't the safest city."

Cory leaned down, kissed Jonathan, and said, "I will."

Jonathan went back to sleep for another two hours. He was about to get up when Cory returned to the room.

"Guess what? I ran into Forrest Woodward downstairs. He offered to take me to breakfast, but I told him I wanted to see how you were doing."

Jonathan knew Woodward's appearance was not a coincidence. He also knew the man was trying to make a move on Cory. Jonathan offered a cold smile as he shook his head. "Let's let Cal deal with Woodward."

"He said he wanted to work with us."

Jonathan stared at Cory for a long moment. "No, Cory, he wants to work with you, and his interest isn't professional."

Cory looked stunned. "Are you sure? He knows I'm with you."

"Yes, I'm sure. It was obvious back in San Francisco."

"I think he's waiting for us downstairs."

"Well, let's go meet the man."

Cory had the feeling things were not going to go well, as she followed Jonathan out of the room.

Forrest was sitting on a bench across the lobby from the elevators. He rose to meet the couple.

"Morning, why don't we find somewhere private to talk about our plans?"

Neither Jonathan nor Cory responded as they followed Woodward across the lobby and into a room with scattered chairs and tables set up for private conversations. One man was by himself, reading a book, otherwise, the room was empty. The agent led them to a quiet corner across the room from the reader.

Once seated, he turned his attention to Jonathan and Cory. "So, what's the plan? How are we going to investigate the nine people on your list?"

Jonathan leaned forward. "We aren't going to investigate them; Cory and I will be investigating them."

Woodward seemed startled, a puzzled expression on his face. "What are you talking about, this is my investigation. I'm running this show."

Jonathan leaned back in his chair. "No, Agent Woodward. Cory and I work alone. Cal Hulse will keep you informed."

Woodward's face flushed and his body tensed. "No way. If I'm not involved completely, it's not happening. You don't like it, you're out." He turned to Cory. "Who are we going to look at first?"

Cory shook her head and said, "You are the one who doesn't seem to get the picture. Jonathan and I are together in more ways than one. Accept that or we'll be booking our return flight."

When there was no response, Jonathan and Cory stood up and left the room.

CHAPTER 12

As they were seated in the hotel dining room, Cory said, "Well, that went well."

Jonathan smiled, reached across the table, and patted Cory's hand. "Actually, it went exceedingly well. I don't think Agent Woodward will be bothering us."

Cory looked up from the breakfast menu. "So, what's our plan?"

"I don't have a clue, but we'll come up with something."

Later, in their hotel room, they mulled over how to approach their nine possible suspects.

Cory was becoming increasingly frustrated. "We're not going to get anywhere by directly confronting these people; they'll either deny being the source of the leaks or refuse to talk to us."

Jonathan nodded in agreement. After a few moments, he looked up, his eyes bright as an idea came to him. "The word has to be out that the Defense Intelligence Agency is performing an investigation. About forty people are under the agency's microscope. Since the common thread is their contact with the Taiwan defense plans, they've probably figured out the reason for the investigation."

When Jonathan paused, Cory said, "Okay, but how does that help us?"

"What if we approached each person on the list and asked for their help?"

"Their help?"

"Yeah, ask each person who they think would most likely be the leaker."

Cory gave a tentative smile. "We don't have the credentials to do that. We're not agency personnel."

"Call Woodward. Tell him we need the type of credentials that would authorize us to question the people."

"You want me to call him?"

"You would have a better chance to have him agree. I'm not his flavor of the month."

Cory picked up her phone and made the call. Jonathan could only hear her side of the conversation, but it was obvious the agent was saying, no."

At one point, Cory said, "If we don't have the authority to make these people talk to us, why are we here? Give us the credentials, or we're out of here."

Several moments passed as Cory listened, without speaking. When she finally hung up, she turned to Jonathan and said, "He'll give me the credentials, but not you."

"Well, that means I can't be with you if we do the approach at their workplaces. If we do it somewhere else, we can probably bluff them about my presence."

"I don't want to question these people without you."

"Let's think about that."

Cory's credentials arrived via messenger the following day. They selected Colonel Susan Giambruno as their first interviewee, not because they thought her to be the most likely leaker, but for the opposite reason. They believed the colonel to be one of the least likely, and therefore someone they could use to practice and refine their interviewing skills.

They waited until six o'clock in the evening and approached her off-base apartment without calling ahead.

When Giambruno answered the door, she was still wearing her dress uniform and a wary expression.

"Can I help you?"

Cory flashed her new credentials. "We're working with the Defense Intelligence Agency, and would like to ask you a few questions."

"Can I see those credentials?"

Cory handed her creds to the colonel and stood silently as the woman closely reviewed the document. When the woman looked up, she said, "What is this about?"

"Can we discuss this inside?"

When Giambruno hesitated, Cory said, "If you prefer, we can escort you to our office."

After a moment's hesitation, she waved them inside.

The apartment was very neat, but had the appearance of somewhat temporary accommodations. Jonathan and Cory remained standing in the living room until the colonel took a seat. They settled onto a sofa opposite the woman.

Susan Giambruno was a tanned, brown-haired woman just over thirty years of age. Her features were attractive, but a bit on the cold, hard side. Her body had the look of someone who worked out regularly.

Jonathan smiled as he said, "We're not here to investigate you. As I'm sure you're aware, information has been leaking out of the DOD. Do you have any idea who may be doing the leaking?"

The woman seemed genuinely stunned by the question. "God, no."

Jonathan handed the colonel a sheet of paper. "This is a list of people who had access to the leaked information. Could you take a look at it?" He handed her the sheet of paper. The list did not include her name.

After a few moments, she shook her head. "I only know a few of these people. I can't believe any of them would be leaking classified information."

"That's fine. Can you tell us the names that you recognize?"

"Well, General Hamlin is my commanding officer, and I work with Colonel Nunemann. I cannot believe these people would be leaking information."

Cory spoke up. "How well do you know the two people you mentioned?"

Giambruno sat back in her chair and gave the question some thought.

"I know General Hamlin very well. I have to say, I haven't had any contact with Colonel Nunemann outside of the office."

Cory stood up and offered the colonel her hand. "Thank you so much for your cooperation." Jonathan stood and offered his hand.

As Cory started moving toward the door, she turned toward Colonel Giambruno, "I'm sure you're aware of the sensitive nature of our investigation. Please keep our meeting completely confidential."

When the colonel did not respond. Cory stopped and studied the woman for a moment. "Do you understand what I just said?"

Giambruno stammered, "Of course."

On the way back to their car, Cory asked, "What do you think?"

"She's either the best actress I've ever seen, or she's not our leaker."

"I agree."

CHAPTER 13

The weather had changed dramatically, from cool, clear days to threatening skies. Jonathan and Cory huddled in their hotel room with room service dinners as they considered their next move. With eight to go, they agreed no one officer was a better prospect than the next.

They decided to call on General William Barron in the morning, followed by Colonel Raymond Handy. That decided, their focus shifted to the bedroom for recreational activities.

The following day was a Saturday, and they assumed most of the eight men on the list would be home. Their GPS led them to a two-story, wood-shingled townhouse in an upscale neighborhood.

Jonathan rang the doorbell and stepped back behind Cory, who had her credentials at the ready. A tall, attractive woman in her midsixties opened the door, flanked by an enormous dog. Both Jonathan and Cory stepped back slightly at the sight of the dog.

The woman smiled. "Don't worry, Doris is friendly. Can I help you?"

Cory continued staring at Dorris as she produced her credentials. "We're with the Defense Intelligence Agency and would like to speak with General Barron."

"Can I ask what this is about?"

"I'm afraid the matter is classified, but we're hoping the general can assist us in our investigation."

The woman paused, as if undecided, then opened the door all the way and motioned them inside. "I'm Joy Barron, Bill's wife."

They followed the woman into her living room. "Please take a seat, Bill's in his study. I'll tell him you're here."

When she left the room, Doris, a one hundred twenty-pound Irish Wolfhound, gave Cory a sniff and then stood in front of Jonathan. Not sure of the outcome, he slowly reached down and began rubbing the dog's ears. Doris seemed to smile as she wagged her tail.

A large man walked into the room and studied his guests. "General Barron. Can I see your credentials?"

Cory stepped forward and handed him her cred packet. The general put on a pair of reading glasses and examined the document. "Very well. What is this about?"

Cory said, "We're conducting an investigation and would like your help. Can we sit down?"

The general's expression was still wary as he handed Cory her credentials and motioned them toward a seating arrangement. Cory and Jonathan took seats on a sofa while Barron sat in a facing chair. Doris placed her large head in Jonathan's lap, which seemed to somehow relax the general.

Cory took the lead. "General, I'm sure you're aware that sensitive information has been leaking, most probably to the Chinese." She handed the general a sheet of paper. "These are people who had access to the leaked information. We'd like you to look at the list and tell us what you know about any of the officers you're familiar with." Naturally, General Barron's name was not on the list.

The general took the list and glanced at it. "Look, I'm not comfortable doing this."

Jonathan gave an understanding smile and said, "Perhaps you could tell us which people you know that could be eliminated from consideration."

Barron thought for a moment, then again studied the list. "I work with General Cannon, and Colonel Doherty reports to me. I also know

General Kelly. I can't believe any of these officers would reveal classified material to our adversary."

Jonathan made notes as the general spoke. Realizing they had obtained all the information Barron was willing to share, Cory stood and offered his hand. The general seemed startled that the interview was over as he stood and shook her hand.

"General, this matter is highly confidential. Please do not discuss our meeting with anyone."

"Of course." When he glanced at Jonathan, he said, "I see Doris has made a new friend."

"She's a beautiful dog."

"Member of the family."

As they walked to their car, Cory said, "We didn't gain any useful information."

"No, but my opinion is that the general is a straight shooter. Nice home, but nothing out of the range of a general's salary."

Their navigation system led them to Colonel Raymond Handy's home, which turned out to be a condominium on the third floor of a large complex on the bank of the Potomac River. Jonathan assumed the units with a view of the river would be the most desirable, and therefore, the most expensive.

When they buzzed the colonel's condo, there was no answer. The colonel was either not in, or not accepting visitors. Undeterred, Jonathan and Cory returned to their car, pulled out a file, and programmed their GPS to guide them to General James Farrell's address.

This took them to Arlington, Virginia, and a neighborhood named Broyhill Forest. The general's home was a mini mansion on North Vermont Street. Cory and Jonathan sat in their car and stared at the structure.

Cory said, "I think they call this a Georgian architectural style."

"I call it a lot of money."

"The information from Cal didn't pick up on Farrell being loaded."

Jonathan shook his head as he looked at the general's home. "No. This could be interesting."

When they rang, the door was opened by a middle-aged Hispanic woman. She stood and stared at Jonathan and Cory before saying, "Yes?"

Cory stepped forward. "We would like to speak with General Farrell."

"Do you have an appointment?"

"No, we do not. Please tell the general that we are from the Defense Intelligence Agency."

"One moment, please." The woman closed the door. Cory and Jonathan looked at each other, wondering if the woman would return.

Several minutes later, the woman opened the door and said, "Please follow me."

They stepped into a large, high-ceilinged entry. Their footsteps echoed off the polished stone floor. The woman led them to a huge living room, dominated by a stone fireplace. A moment later, a man dressed in slacks and a polo shirt entered the room. The man was in his late fifties, of medium height, and with the wiry build of a man in excellent shape.

"I'm General James Farrell. That will be all, Carmen." The woman turned and left the room. "What is this about?"

Cory stepped forward and offered her credentials. "We're from the Defense Intelligence Agency and would like your assistance in an investigation we're conducting."

The general paused before accepting Cory's creds. He carefully examined the document before handing it back. "Again, what is this about?"

The general's expression and body language were not welcoming. Cory smiled and asked, "Can we sit down, general? We only have a few questions, and we'd like your assistance."

Farrell took a moment to respond, as if he was debating telling them to leave. He finally motioned toward a seating area.

When they were settled, Cory said, "General, I'm sure you're aware that sensitive information has been leaked from the DOD. We would like you to look at a list of individuals who had access to that information and tell us anything you can about the officers that you know."

Cory opened her briefcase, extracted a file, and handed the general a single sheet of paper.

Farrell leaned back in his chair and held up his hand, as if to ward off the paper. "No. I'm not going to cooperate."

Jonathan stood up. "Fine, General. We thought an informal meeting with you was the way to go, but I'm sure Forrest Woodward at the DIA can set up a meeting in a more formal setting."

As Cory stood up to join Jonathan, the general waved them back. "All right, let me see your information."

Cory handed Farrell the list. He studied it for several minutes. "I know General Kelly and General Cannon, and Colonel Handy reports to me. I don't believe any of these men would be responsible for the leaks."

Cory stood up, retrieved the list, and said, "Thank you, General. This investigation is highly classified. Please don't discuss this meeting with anyone."

Farrell appeared surprised. "That's it?"

"Yes, general. Thank you for meeting with us."

He stood and followed them out of the room and opened the front door. Neither Jonathan nor Cory spoke until they were in their car. Cory glanced back at the house. "So far, the three we talked to thought none of the people they know could be the leaker."

"I know. We need Cal to find out how the general can afford a home worth several million."

CHAPTER 14

As soon as they were back at their hotel, Jonathan called Cal. As usual, it went to voicemail. He noted in his message that it was important. He then went online looking for dinner reservations.

Jonathan glanced over at Cory as she was studying the bios of the remaining six people on their list. "How about dinner at the Capital Grill at the Capitol?"

"Sounds appropriate."

"Well, reservations are at seven thirty. We have some time to kill. What do you feel like doing?"

This brought a smile. "We can either watch C-SPAN or make love, you're call."

Jonathan pretended to ponder the question for about five seconds.

They were about to be seated at the restaurant when Jonathan's phone chirped. A quick glance at the screen showed Cal was the caller. Jonathan excused himself and went back to the lobby to take the call.

"Hey, Jon. A breakthrough in the investigation?

"Maybe. The bio on James Farrell didn't mention anything about his being wealthy, but his house has to be worth several million. He even has a full-time maid."

There was a pause as Cal thought about Jonathan's comment. "No, nothing like that was in the information from Woodward. Let me look into it."

"Okay. We're about to have dinner. Call me when you have something."

When he returned to the table, Cory gave him a questioning look. "Cal, returning my call. He's going to dig into the general's finances."

Cory and Jonathan ordered glasses of Pine Ridge Chardonnay as they studied their menus. When the waiter returned with their wine, Cory ordered the sushi-rubbed seared sesame tuna while Jonathan went with the bone-in ribeye, medium rare, and a bottle of Cardinale Cabernet.

At one point, Cory paused and asked, "Do you think Farrell's wealth came from selling classified information?"

Jonathan took a moment before he shook his head. "It's too obvious. Everyone must know he has a lot of money, but we have to keep turning over rocks until we find the answer."

"So, who's next on the list?"

"Let's give Colonel Handy another try, and I'm interested in Colonel Doherty who has a lot of debt."

The following morning, there was a response when they buzzed Colonel Raymond Handy's condominium. A man's voice came through a speaker near the door. "Hello, who's there?"

When Cory responded, there was a pause before the voice said, "All right, unit 405."

After being buzzed into the building, they took the elevator to the fourth floor. Jonathan noticed the condo was not facing the Potomac.

The man answering the door was taller than Jonathan, had a pale Irish complexion, and was quite thin. He was dressed in tan pants and a polo shirt. His expression was anything but friendly.

"What is this about? Look, I have a nine o'clock tee time."

Cory said, "We'll only need about fifteen minutes. Can we come in?"

The colonel reluctantly stepped aside. "You said you're with the Defense Intelligence Agency. Can I see your credentials?"

Cory handed over her creds. After studying her credentials, he said, "Like I said, I was just about to leave."

Cory's voice stiffened. "And like I said, we'll be out in fifteen minutes. Someone at the DOD is leaking information." She pulled a sheet of paper from her briefcase. "This is a list of people who had access to that information. Please look at the list and tell us anything you know regarding them."

Still standing in the condominium's entry, he took the list. After a moment, he said, "Well, of course, I know General Farrell. I report to him. I often work with Colonel Doherty. I'm quite sure neither Farrell or Doherty would be leaking information."

Jonathan spoke up, "Colonel, why are you sure?"

Handy gave Jonathan a look of pure n exasperation. "Because I know these men."

Cory stepped in and retrieved the list. "Thank you, Colonel. Please don't discuss this meeting with anyone. As I'm sure you are aware, this matter is highly classified."

Five minutes later, they were in their car heading for Colonel Thomas Doherty's address, which turned out to be a somewhat shopworn apartment building in Arlington, Virginia. Unlike the homes of the other officers they had talked to, this building had no security. They walked up to the second floor and knocked on the colonel's door.

With a name like Doherty, Jonathan expected to see a ruddy-faced, pale-complexioned man of Irish descent. The man who opened the door was a dark-skinned black man.

"Yes?"

Cory took the lead. "Colonel Doherty, we're from the Defense Intelligence Agency. Could we have a few minutes of your time?"

"What is this about?" The colonel's accent was definitely from the Deep South.

"Can we come in. We'd rather not discuss this in your hallway."

"Your credentials."

Cory handed them to the colonel. After a moment's hesitation, he stepped back and motioned them into his apartment. Once inside the unit, he turned and asked in an unfriendly tone, "All right, now, why are you here?"

Cory gave the now-practiced explanation. Doherty listened, then said, "I have no idea who is leaking classified information. When Cory produced her list of eight officers, he pushed it away. This is bullshit. Please leave."

"We report to a man named Forrest Woodward at the DIA. I'm sure he'll be in touch." That said, Cory placed the list back in her briefcase and headed toward the door, with Jonathan following.

As they walked back to their car, Cory turned to Jonathan. "What do you think?"

"If he's the leaker, he's not making any money at it. Shabby apartment in a not great neighborhood. His furniture looks like it came from Goodwill."

"A lot of anger. Maybe pissed off at the DOD."

"Maybe. Let's have Cal do some digging." He looked at his watch. "Doherty certainly didn't take any time. Let's hit one more. I'm interested in Seth Cannon, who recently bought an expensive home."

The GPS led them to Old Gate Court in McLean, Virginia. They parked in front of a large, contemporary home. They studied the home for several minutes. Jonathan said, "Has to be at least four thousand square feet, and it looks like a double lot."

They marched up the path from the street and rang the doorbell. Jonathan noticed a security camera covering the area around the front door. A voice came from a hidden speaker. "We do not accept solicitations."

Cory held her credentials up to the camera. "We're with the Defense Intelligence Agency."

There was a pause before the front door opened. A trim man with short cut, graying hair gave them a quizzical look. "The DIA? How can I help you?"

Cory smiled and said, "I'll be happy to tell you, can we come in?"

"Of course." The general stepped back. They entered a beautifully furnished home. The furnishings were a mixture of very modern decor with a sprinkling of items that the general must have collected from his foreign postings.

Jonathan looked around, obviously impressed. "General, beautiful home. Did you win the lottery?"

The man laughed. "Almost, I took a flyer on Bitcoin when it first came out."

When they were seated in the general's living room, Cory described the leaks from the DOD and handed General Cannon the list of people who had access to the leaked information.

The general studied the list for several moments. "I work with General Barron and General Farrell, and I know Colonel Nunemann and Colonel Giambruno. I can't believe any of these people would betray their country."

He handed the list back to Cory. She stood up, shook the general's hand, and told the man not to discuss the information she had shared with anyone.

Cal called Jonathan while they were driving back to their hotel. "Jon, General Farrell isn't rich; his wife is. Sally Farrell is part of the Mars family, which is valued at $117 billion."

"Okay, I guess the general doesn't need Chinese money. We ran into a problem when we called on Colonel Doherty. He's obviously hurting financially, and he refused to talk to us. He came across as a very angry man."

"I'll look into it. Has anything interesting come up?"

"No, and we're running out of people to talk to."

Jonathan turned to Cory and shook his head. "Cal checked out Farrell. It turns out his wife has a ton of family money."

Corry's expression was grim. "Only three left on the list. The home team isn't scoring any runs."

"No, the only one who stands out is Doherty, and if he's it, he's a very poorly paid leaker."

"Well, they'll all be at work tomorrow, and since Woodward wouldn't give you credentials, we can only talk to them when they're home in the evening."

Jonathan nodded. "I've never been to Washington before. How about you?"

When Cory shook her head, he said, "Tomorrow, let's play tourist. Tour the White House, the Lincoln Memorial, all that stuff."

This brought out a smile. "Sounds like fun."

CHAPTER 15

Cal called Jonathan, and Cory was about to leave their hotel.

"Jon, I just got a call from Woodward. Apparently, the word is out that you're interviewing people at the Department of Defense about the leaks."

"I can't say I'm surprised. We cautioned everyone not to discuss our meetings with anyone, but I guess it's hard to keep a secret in Washington."

"No doubt. How do you think it'll affect the ones you haven't talked to?"

Jonathan thought for a moment. "They probably know we're coming, but I don't know if it really changes anything."

They were in the back seat of an Uber on the way to the White House when Cory looked over at Jonathan. "Have you called your folks? Is Bo doing okay?"

Jonathan smiled. "He's doing fine. Apparently, he sat, staring at the front door the day I left, but now he's adjusted to the change." Jonathan laughed, "Dad said they don't want to give him back to me."

They stood in a long line to tour the White House and were somewhat disappointed with the limited access the tour provided. Jonathan and Cory then walked over to the Lincoln Memorial and the Reflecting Pool. After lunch, they visited the Vietnam Memorial.

Cory turned to Jonathan on the ride back to their hotel. "I'm really glad we did this. I thought the Lincoln Memorial was fantastic."

Jonathan nodded, his mood affected by the Vietnam Memorial. "So many died in that senseless war."

Cory realized how the memorial had affected Jonathan. Trying to turn his mind to their investigation she asked, "Who's next on the list?"

Jonathan shrugged, "It really doesn't matter, two generals and a colonel. Your pick."

"Let's go with one of the generals."

The visit to General William Hamlin's townhouse in Arlington offered no useful information. While cordial, the general acknowledged that Colonel Susan Giambruno was a direct report and that he was a friend of General Michael Kelly, he was certain that neither officer was leaking information. In passing, he mentioned that he would be retiring in the coming year at which time he and his wife would be moving back to Texas.

The meeting with Hamlin was so brief that Jonathan and Cory decided it was early enough to call on General Kelly. The general's home turned out to be a large two-story red brick home in Fairfax Station, Virginia.

When they parked in front of the home, Jonathan glanced at Cory, "This has to be worth a great deal."

"Not as much as you might think. I looked at homes for sale in the area, and it's probably in the $800,000 area. We're not in California."

"No kidding, if this place were in a decent neighborhood in the city, it would be worth over two million."

The front door opened before they had a chance to ring the doorbell. No doubt their presence was picked up by a camera system. The man standing in the doorway was in his midfifties and had the build of a middle linebacker. His close-cut hair and erect posture left no question about his military background.

Cory stepped forward. "General Kelly, I'm Cory Bishop, and I'm with the Defense Intelligence Agency."

When Cory offered her credentials, the general waved them off. "I was expecting you. Please come in."

"You were expecting us?"

General Kelly laughed as he led them into his home. "Yes, the word's out. Can I offer you anything, coffee, water, or a Coke?"

Cory and Jonathan declined and sat on a sofa with the general in a facing chair.

"General, since you were expecting us, you are probably aware of why we're here. Information has been leaking, and it's believed to be coming from someone at the DOD." She handed the general the list. "These are people who have had access to the information."

Kelly glanced at the list and shook his head as he handed it back. "I know several of the officers on your list, and there is no way any of them would sell out their country."

"Well, general, someone is."

The general's expression hardened. "I'm sure you're right. I just don't believe it's someone on your list."

Jonathan spoke for the first time. "If it's not someone on this list, any ideas where we should be looking?"

General Kelly sat back and thought for a moment. "Not really. Have you considered some type of cyber intrusion?"

Jonathan paused before he said, "We're working with a highly skilled IT expert. I'll ask him, but I have to assume your systems are quite secure."

When they were back in their car, Jonathan turned to Cory. "You think it's possible the Pentagon's systems got hacked?"

"I would think Woodward's people would have been all over that possibility."

CHAPTER 16

The latest thumb drive Allen Chen retrieved from under the park bench did not contain DOD classified information. It simply informed Chen that a man and woman from the Defense Intelligence Agency were interviewing several senior people regarding leaks from the Pentagon. It also stated that, while he did not believe they had talked to General Kelly, he would certainly be on the list.

The news was not surprising. Chen had been aware of the so far ineffective efforts by the DIA to uncover the source of the leaked information. Nevertheless, Chen passed Wu's information on to his controller.

It took two days for the controller's sources to uncover the names of the investigators: Cory Bishop and Jonathan Scanlan. The names meant nothing to the controller, but he passed the information on to Beijing. Within a day, the CCP linked Cory Bishop and Jonathan Scanlan, along with Cal Hulse, to the destruction of the Independence Corporation, a highly secretive defense contractor in Austin, Texas. Jonathan's most recent book, *The Independence Conspiracy*, described how the contractor had been revealed to be wholly owned by the Chinese government.

Suddenly, Beijing considered Jonathan, Cory, and, no doubt, Cal's investigation as a serious threat. The controller was given instructions to place the three under constant surveillance and to report their activities daily. When Jonathan and Cory left their hotel room the following morning, listening devices were installed in their room.

The team assigned to monitor Cal Hulse found their task to be more difficult. Access to his condominium presented several problems. The building had excellent security, and his government supplied computer and communication systems were virtually hack-proof. The fact that he worked from home also limited his opportunity to access his unit. Even exterior surveillance was a problem. Asian men sitting in a car outside an expensive condo in Pacific Heights for an extended period of time would invite a police inquiry.

Consideration was given to eliminating Hulse, Scanlan, and Bishop, but it was decided that such action was premature. It did not appear that their investigation was bearing any fruit and would very likely be discontinued.

When Jonathan and Cory went downstairs to the hotel dining room for breakfast, an attractive Asian couple was seated at a nearby table. Jonathan noticed them, but gave no importance to their presence.

With little to do until interviewing Colonel Robert Nunemann, the last officer on their list, Jonathan and Cory decided to take a river cruise on the Potomac. The weather was cooperating, with clear skies as they arrived at the Potomac Riverboat docks.

The riverboat was comfortable as it moved upriver at a leisurely pace. A guide pointed out the various sites of interest as they cruised past the nation's capital. Jonathan noticed the same Asian couple he had seen earlier that morning at their hotel. While not given to conspiracy theories, he had trouble dismissing their presence as a coincidence.

As they were disembarking, he leaned down and whispered in Cory's ear. "There's an attractive Asian couple behind us. They were seated near us this morning at breakfast."

When Cory started to turn around, he said, "Don't look at them. Let's see if they follow us when we leave."

When they reached their rental and drove out of the parking lot, the couple followed, two cars behind, in a dark blue Toyota Camry. Jonathan gave Cory a tight smile. "Let's take the scenic route back to the hotel."

After twenty minutes, it became obvious that they were being followed. Cory seemed more concerned than Jonathan. "What should we do about it?"

Jonathan shrugged. "I'm not sure. Let's go back to the hotel and call Cal. He can let Woodward know. Maybe he'll have an idea."

When they reached their hotel, Jonathan called Cal before leaving the car. As usual, it went to voicemail. He left a message, describing the situation and asking for Woodward's advice. An hour later, Cal returned the call.

"Hi Jon. I talked to Woodward, and he said he's not surprised they have you under surveillance. He also said that they've probably bugged your room."

That gave Jonathan a moment to think about what he and Cory might have said in the room that would be a problem. Since they had no idea who was leaking the information, he dismissed the thought.

"All right. We only have Colonel Nunemann to talk to. After that, if nothing pops, we might as well head home."

"By the way, I checked out Doherty. He was pretty much wiped out by an ugly divorce."

"I guess that would be enough to piss you off, but it also doesn't eliminate him."

Later, that evening, they drove to Alexandra. The colonel's condominium was in a well-tended three-story complex. When they were buzzed in and greeted at the door, it was obvious the colonel had been expecting them.

"Good evening, Colonel. We're from the Defense Intelligence Agency, and we'd like a few minutes of your time." Cory offered her credentials."

"Please come in." Colonel Nunemann's attitude seemed more resigned than unfriendly. Cory gave him the now-standard spiel, which solicited virtually no reaction. When she handed the list of officers that had received the leaked information, the colonel glanced at the list and, immediately, handed it back to Cory.

"I don't believe any of the people on this list would betray their country."

"Colonel, someone is leaking the information. If not the people on this list, then who?"

"Look, I'm not saying classified information is not being leaked. I just don't believe these people are responsible."

They sat in an awkward silence for a moment before Jonathan and Cory stood up, thanked Nunemann for his time, and left the unit. When they were back in their car, Jonathan shook his head. "Well, we're zero for nine."

Cory did not answer, but her expression showed agreement. Jonathan noticed a dark colored sedan that followed them back to their hotel.

CHAPTER 17

When they reached their hotel, they requested a room change. When the desk clerk asked why they wanted the change, they shrugged and said they simply wanted a different room. The clerk did not pursue it and provided a new set of electronic keys. Jonathan told him they would be out of their old room in thirty minutes.

Once settled in their new room, Jonathan stared out the large window in their sitting area as he thought about their lack of progress and what might be their next move. After a while, he turned to Cory. "Maybe I'm not the best judge of character, but none of the nine people gave me a bad guy vibe."

Cory was pulling a small bottle from the minibar. "I agree. While none of them wanted to be interviewed, all but Doherty seemed clean."

"Yeah, and I don't believe he's the leaker. He'd be living better if he were selling secrets."

"So, back to SF?"

"Let's take a day to think about it. Maybe we can come up with a new game plan."

The following morning, when they arrived for breakfast and different Asian couple came in behind them and took a nearby table. Jonathan stared at them for a moment before turning to Cory.

"You think we should ask them to join us?"

His comment brought out a smile. "I don't think so."

"I have an idea. I'll tell you when we're back in our room. For all I know, these characters can read lips."

"Do you think they might be bugging our room while we're here?'

"I doubt it, but you're right. Let's not gamble on it. We'll find somewhere private after breakfast."

When they left the restaurant, they walked to the back of the hotel to the pool area. The cool weather had left the area deserted. They settled in at a small table with facing chairs.

"Okay, what's your idea?"

"We create a false story to be leaked, but limit the number of people who have access. I mean, way less than the nine, and see if China reacts."

Cory sat back and thought about the idea, "And if China doesn't react, those people could be eliminated."

"We could do this more than once."

"Woodward would have to go for it."

Jonathan nodded. "I know. The leak would have to be something serious enough to force a reaction, but not a Chinese overreaction."

Cory was smiling when she said, "I like it. Give Cal a call."

Jonathan made the call, which went to voicemail, and left a message for a call back.

When Cal eventually called back, Jonathan told him about his plan. Cal took a moment to consider the idea. "I'll have to talk to Woodward."

"If he doesn't go for it, I don't see any reason for us to hang out in DC."

"I understand, but even if he agrees, it'll take some time to put it together."

"I'm sure you're right. Why don't we head home? We can always come back here."

"All right. I'll call you after I talk to him."

Two hours later, Jonathan's phone chirped. "It took some prodding, but he went for it. He said it would probably take a week to come up with the plan and put it in place."

"Okay, we'll be flying home tomorrow."

CHAPTER 18

The flight home was uneventful. Cory popped her pills and slept the entire way. Jonathan alternated between reading a new book by John Sanford and watching an action movie. He woke Cory as they began their descent.

As before, she was groggy as he led her off the plane. Cory had used an Uber ride when she met Jonathan at the airport for their departing flight. Jonathan watched her and knew she was in no shape to make her way home by herself. He guided her to his Jeep and drove her to her condo in San Carlos. Once she was safely in her unit he left and made his way back to his home. He failed to notice the Ford SUV that followed him home.

With the time change, it was midafternoon when he entered his home on Jackson. He had not exercised when he was in Washington and he decided to go for a run. When he crossed the street to enter the Presidio, he did notice two men sitting in an SUV two houses down.

They were still there when he finished his run. After he showered and cleaned up, he called Cal and left a message telling him he was being watched.

Jonathan booked a flight to St. George for the following day and called his parents to tell them his arrival time. As he sat at his desk, he thought about Woodward's advice about his hotel room being bugged. If they could place listening devices in his hotel room, why would they not place them in his home? His home security was limited to an alarm system that he rarely activated.

After he gave it a few more minutes of thought, he walked out of the house and into his backyard. Once outside, he used his cell to call Myron Rossi. The big man answered on the second ring.

"Jonathan, great to hear from you. How are things going?"

"I'm fine, but there's a chance my house has been bugged. Do you know someone who can check it out for me?"

"Hell, I can do that. Why do you think your place might be bugged?"

"It's complicated, but I'll tell you all about it when I see you. I'm flying to Utah tomorrow to see my parents and pick up Bo. Could you come up here on Friday or Saturday?"

"Sure, Friday would work. Should I bring my anti-bad-guy equipment?"

"I don't think you'll need your tools, but bring them along."

Jonathan smiled as he thought about Myron. Jonathan had basically blackmailed the FBI into arranging for Myron to obtain a private investigator's license at the conclusion of the Independence affair. After he recovered from being shot, the big man set up a solo practice in Los Angeles.

Jonathan's flight to St. George was on time and uneventful. His father was waiting to greet him once he cleared the restricted area of the terminal. The two men embraced in an awkward hug, neither being the hugging type.

Jonathan's father was smiling like a child on Christmas morning. "How was your trip to Washington?"

"The trip was fine. Cory and I had quite a bit of free time, so we toured the White House and visited all the big sights."

"That's great. Your mother was hoping Cory would be with you."

Jonathan smiled, patted his father on the shoulder, and led the way out of the terminal. Thomas Scanlan had driven Jonathan's Jeep to the airport, and when they approached it, Bo began jumping up and down in the back.

Jonathan's father was smiling when he said, "Someone's happy to see you."

CHAPTER 19

It took Jonathan a day to recover from the long, boring drive back to San Francisco. Myron arrived late Friday in his Lincoln Continental, a byproduct of the Independence adventure. Once inside the house, he brought out a device and began scanning the house from top to bottom.

When he was finished, he motioned for Jonathan to step outside. "I found four listening devices. They were in your kitchen, living room, bedroom, and office. There's also a tap on your landline. I assume you would want me to get rid of them."

Jonathan ran his hand through his hair as he thought about the advantages of leaving them in place. He finally shook his head. "Take out the bugs, but let's leave the phone alone. Can you tell if my computer has been compromised?"

"That's beyond me. You'll have to bring in a techy for that."

"I'll call Cal. I'm sure he knows someone who can handle that."

Myron sat down on one of Jonathan's patio chairs. "So, whose doing this?"

Jonathan again paused, thinking about Woodward's warnings. After a moment, he thought, screw Woodward, Myron had saved his life more than once. "The Chinese."

Myron was clearly taken aback. "Holy shit, you mean the communist Chinese?"

"I can't tell you the details, but Cal, Cory, and I have been working on something for the Defense Intelligence Agency."

The big man was silent for a moment. "Well, I'll take care of the bugs, but you need to seriously upgrade your security system. The locks on your doors also need to be upgraded. Do you need protection?"

"No, at least not right now. As far as security, I'm sure you know a lot more than I do on that. Will you take care of it? Of course, I'm happy to pay you for your time."

Myron shook his head. "You take care of the outside costs, but I don't need to be paid. I'd still be hired muscle for the loan shark if it wasn't for you."

"Thanks, but I insist."

"Well, let me bring in my gear and get started. Can I use the same bedroom as before?"

"Of course."

Cory came up to the city the following day and joined Jonathan and Myron. Myron was unsure how to handle himself when Cory hugged him and kissed his cheek. Jonathan decided to prepare a dinner for his friends and called Cal, who was quick to accept.

Jonathan had taken up cooking during the Independence investigation. Initially, he began preparing dinners to have something to do. It turned out he enjoyed the process and was quite good at it.

When Cal arrived shortly after five, Myron beamed. "Hey, look, the bands back together."

After cocktails, they trooped into the dining room where they were served bruschetta with prosciutto as an appetizer, followed by roast beef and Yorkshire pudding accompanied by potatoes with garlic. The dessert was a store-bought peach pie. Cory, not a big red meat consumer, asked for a small cut of the roast beef but was pleased with her dinner.

Everyone was interested in Myron's private eye business, pressing him for details on his more interesting cases and clients.

Sunday, Cory, Jonathan, and Myron lounged around during the

morning. Later, Cory joined Jonathan and Bo for a brief run in the Presidio while Myron was content with a stroll through the neighborhood. When they saw two men in a car a few houses down the street, Myron offered to brace them, but Jonathan told him to leave them alone.

Early Monday morning, the security people arrived. After four hours, a state-of-the-art security system was installed, which covered both front and rear doors and ground-level windows. Exterior cameras were installed covering the front entrance and rear of the house. A locksmith replaced the locks on the exterior doors. Jonathan, who was not technically proficient, required another half hour to understand how to operate the systems.

Myron had supervised the installation of the security systems. When the technicians left, Myron decided to head home. He turned to Jonathan as he was about to leave. "If things start to get hairy, call me."

Jonathan patted the big man on his shoulder. "Don't worry, I will."

After Myron had left, Jonathan went to his office and called the number Cal had given him, using his cell. A man with a Midwest accent answered.

"Hall Cyber Security."

"Hi, my name is Jonathan Scanlan. Cal Hulse gave me your number. I need to know if my computer system has been compromised."

"Where are you?"

"San Francisco."

"Okay, I'm in Burlingame. What's your schedule like tomorrow?"

"I'm fine for tomorrow."

"Give me your address. I'll be there at eleven."

Jonatha gave the man his address, feeling he had covered all the bases. Bo had been sitting next to him. Jonathan bent down and said, "Want to go for a run?"

Bo ran to where his leash was resting on the kitchen counter.

CHAPTER 20

A week later, Cal called Jonathan as he was at his desk, paying bills. Cal knew the plan was to use Jonathan's land line for normal conversations and his cell for anything related to the leaks.

" I just got a call from Woodward. The story is a plan to move the USS Dwight D Eisenhower to the Taiwan Straits. Only Barron, Cannon, and Doherty received the brief."

"Okay, so now we wait to see if the Chinese react."

"Exactly."

A week later, Jonathan's cell chirped. "Hi, no reaction by the Chinese."

"All right, so we can cross the two generals and the colonel off the list. What happens next?"

"There'll be another briefing for two or three of our candidates in a few days."

This time, the fake briefing went to Hamlin, Nunemann and Giambruno. Again, there was no Chinese response after a six-day wait. The story then went to the remaining three on the list: Kelly, Farrell, and Handy.

Within days, the Chinese navy moved a carrier and two destroyers into the Taiwan Straits.

Cory, Cal, and Jonathan met at Jonathan's bug-free home on Jackson. Jonathan shook his head as he glanced around the room. "I didn't see this coming. All three of these men seemed incapable of slipping this information to our adversary."

Cory nodded in agreement. "Handy was a bit of an asshole, but this is a surprise."

Cal was the only one smiling. "This is great, we've narrowed it down to three potential leakers."

Jonatha stood up and began pacing the room. "I don't know, this just doesn't feel right."

Cal ignored Jonathan's discomfort. "Woodward and his people will be doing a deep dive on these guys."

Cory looked at Cal. "So that's it, we're out of it now?"

Cal shrugged. "Yeah, I guess so. I don't see what else we could do."

Jonathan stopped pacing and sat down. "What about when the USS Dwight D. Eisenhower doesn't move?"

Cal could see where Jonathan was going. Cory said, "What do you mean?"

"These people aren't stupid. When the carrier doesn't start moving toward Taiwan, they're going to know something's wrong."

Cal said, "Maybe Woodward could issue a new briefing. New information caused the plan to be canceled."

"That's a little thin. Especially when a ton of people begin tearing the three officers' lives apart. I think the bad guys can figure out what's really happening."

Cal frowned at his friend. "So what? That will be DIA's problem. We're out of it."

Jonathan had trouble accepting Cal's conclusion. "Maybe. Would anyone else want a drink?"

———

Five men sat at a conference table at the August 1st Building in Beijing, and eight aides stood behind the men at the table. Dong Jun, the Minister of National Defense, glanced across the table at Admiral Hu Zhongming, the head of the Chinese Navy. "Do you agree that the Eisenhour brief was planted to watch our reaction?"

"I'm sure that is the case."

"Who received the brief?"

"Our agent contacted us when Colonel Raymon Handy, General Michael Kelly, and General James Farrell were briefed."

Jun thought for a moment. "Our man reports to Kelly. Their investigation could lead to him."

Chan Wenging, the head of Intelligence, spoke up. "I don't want to pull him out. We have other well-placed valuable assets, but Wu is the best source we have at the Department of Defense."

The minister again paused. "Do we know who created this plan?"

"An agent with the Defense Intelligence Agency named Forrest Woodward issued the brief, but we believe the same people who exposed Independence created the plan."

Jun leaned back in his chair. "Those people caused us a great deal of damage."

Chan Wenging, the most hawkish at the table, spoke forcefully. "We need to eliminate them!"

The minister shook his head. "Perhaps we will, but not immediately. We need misdirection to move attention away from Wu and General Kelly."

The head of Intelligence nodded in agreement. "I suggest we target the colonel. I can have incriminating evidence planted in his home, and possibly on his computer."

Jun offered a cold smile. "Do it."

CHAPTER 21

Ten days later, Woodward called Cal. "We have our leaker." Cal could hear the excitement in the agent's voice. He had no doubt Woodward had taken credit for the plan.

"That's great. Who was it?"

"Colonel Handy."

"How did the agency figure out that he was the one?"

There was a pause, as if Woodward was reluctant to share the details. Finally, he said, "Evidence was found on his personal computer."

"So, it's over."

"Yes, I'll arrange to have the computer and phone we provided picked up."

After Cal hung up, he called Jonathan and relayed the information. "Is this going to be your next book?"

Jonathan thought for a moment. "No, I don't think so. Other than thinking up the fake briefing plan, we didn't do that much. Want to catch dinner?"

"How about tomorrow night?"

"Okay, I'll make a reservation somewhere. Pick you up at seven?"

"I'll be outside."

Jonathan went into the kitchen and pulled a Coke out of the refrigerator. He went to his desk, sat down, and thought about what Cal had told him. Could Colonel Handy really be that stupid to use his home computer to communicate with the CCP? He had not liked the man, but Handy was far from being stupid.

He had a thought. Jonathan went to the front of his home and looked out at the street. He could see two men sitting in a white Honda, watching the house.

The following evening, Jonathan picked up Cal in his Jeep. Cal turned to his friend. "Where are we going?"

"I heard about a place in Richmond named Fiorella Clement. Thought we'd give it a try."

"Sounds good. Italian?"

Jonathan nodded as he drove out of Pacific Heights and into the Richmond District. It took some doing, but they finally found a parking space on Clement, a block from the restaurant.

Jonathan had noticed the white Honda that had followed him from his home. He smiled as he knew they would have a difficult time finding a parking space that they could use to watch his Jeep.

The restaurant turned out to be an upscale bistro. Once settled in at their table, Jonathan ordered a Napa Chardonnay while Cal asked for one of the craft beers.

Cal studied his friend, realizing something was bothering Jonathan. "Is everything all right with Cory?"

The question seemed to startle Jonathan. "Sure, why are you asking?"

"Something's bugging you."

Jonathan took a sip of his wine and nodded. "I'm having trouble seeing Handy as our traitor."

"Why, Woodward said there was evidence on his computer."

"I don't care for the man, but Hardy's a smart guy. Would a smart guy leave incriminating evidence on his computer, knowing he was being investigated? They had no problem getting into my place. I'm sure they could do the same at Handy's condo. Also, if this is all over, why are we still under surveillance?"

Cal was clearly puzzled. "Under surveillance?"

Jonathan nodded. "They've been sitting in a car outside my house, and they followed us here."

"Are you sure?"

"After dinner, I'll introduce you to them."

Cal had no answer as he studied the menu. They both ordered pasta. Jonathan went with spaghetti with mushroom Bolognese, and Cal ordered lasagna puttanesca. At the waiter's suggestion, they ordered a bottle of Barbaresco.

Cal paused halfway through his dinner. "This place is really good. We need to keep it on our list." After a moment, he added, "I have trouble thinking the DIA could be so easily duped."

"Ask our friend Woodward when the evidence was entered on Handy's computer."

"I don't think he'll tell me."

Jonathan thought Cal was probably right.

———

When Jonathan reached home, he glanced at his watch and decided that it was early enough to call Cory. She answered after a few rings, and he could hear her television in the background.

"Hi, let me turn off the movie I was watching. What's up, are we still on for the weekend?"

"Sure, the weekend's fine." He told her about why he had a problem accepting Handy as the leaker.

She did not respond and, for a moment, he thought he had lost the connection. "I don't know. What does Cal think?"

"He believes I'm wrong. I asked him to call Woodward and find out when this evidence entered Handy's computer, but he said he didn't believe Woodward would tell him."

"So, what do you want to do?"

"I don't know."

The following morning, Jonathan's cell chirped just as he was getting out of bed. A glance at the screen showed it was Cory.

"Morning, I wanted to talk to you before I left for work."

"No problem."

"I spent some time last night thinking about what you said. Why don't I call Woodward and ask him about when this stuff went on his computer?"

Jonathan thought for a moment. "I guess it's worth a try. He obviously likes you more than Cal or me. What are you going to say?"

"I haven't thought it through. He's definitely in a self-preservation mode. I'll let you know how it goes."

"Good luck."

CHAPTER 22

Jonathan had watched the evening news and was now staring into his refrigerator, wondering if he could make a dinner out of an array of leftovers when Cory called.

"He said he'd find out the time and date when the information went on his computer."

Jonathan was stunned. "I can't believe Woodward agreed to do that. How did you get him to do that?"

"A little charm and a lot of bullshit."

"Tell me."

"Well, first I stroked his ego. I told him how brilliant *his* plan was to use the fake briefs."

"His plan?"

"I know, but I'm sure he's running around DIA claiming he came up with the idea. I then told him you didn't think Handy was the leaker and planned to continue the investigation on your own. He started screaming about having you prosecuted, when I said, the time and date information would convince you not to go ahead."

"That was it?"

There was a moment's pause. "Well, he suggested we get together on his next trip out here. Don't get upset, I'd rather go out with Kim Jong Un than him."

"Good, my blood pressure was beginning to spike. Let me know after he calls you."

"Of course. What do you want to do on the weekend?"

"I don't know, but I'll think of something."

Cory called the next day during her lunch hour. "Woodward said the entry was made on Saturday, November 1st at 2:12 pm eastern time."

Jonathan checked his records. The entry was made nine days after the false information was provided to the three officers.

Jonathan called Cal and left a message, telling his friend they had to meet. Two hours later, Cal returned the call.

"Why the urgent meeting?"

"Not over the phone. I'll leave for your place right now."

Jonathan rushed out of his house and drove to his friend's condo, with the white Honda following. Once buzzed inside, he took the elevator to Cal's floor. Cal was waiting in the hall. When he started to ask his questions, Jonathan silenced him, led him across the living room and stepped out on the small balcony facing the bay.

When Jonathan slid the sliding glass door closed, Cal reacted as if his friend had lost his mind. "What's this about?"

There were two chairs on the balcony, separated by a small table. Jonathan sat down and motioned Cal toward the other chair.

"Look, I may be overreacting, but you know Myron found four listening devices in my house, and my landline is being tapped. Your security is a great deal better than what I had, but it's possible your condo was also bugged."

This calmed Cal down. "All right, I'll have my place checked out, but what set you off?'

"The incriminating evidence was entered on Handy's computer on November 1st at 2:12 in the afternoon."

Cal was staring at his friend with a blank expression. "So?"

"Think about the timing. That was weeks after Cory and I talked to him and nine days after the fake briefing was circulated to Hardy, Kelly, and Farrell."

Jonathan waited for his information to sink in. "That doesn't mean he didn't enter it."

"Think about it. If he were the leaker, why wouldn't he have entered it and sent it off to Beijing as soon as he received the briefing? Also, this was the only incriminating entry on his computer."

"He could have deleted earlier entries."

"If the pattern was to delete the entries after they were sent, why not this one, and why wait weeks before sending it?"

Cal stared out toward the bay as he mulled over Jonathan's questions. He finally surfaced. "You're right, it stinks. I'm sure the people at the DIA are really smart. Why aren't they picking this up?"

"Maybe some of them are, and maybe not everyone there is doing the victory dance. Woodward is an opportunist, and he was under enormous pressure. He badly wanted a win. It's also possible they saw what we're seeing, and they're just claiming to have uncovered the leaker to buy time."

"Have you talked to Woodward about this?"

"No, but Cory told him what we think.'

"What did he say?"

"He blew her off and told her they have their man."

After a moment Cal looked over at Jonathan. "So, what happens next?"

"We get back at it, and we exclude Woodward. Jonathan looked at his watch. "Cory should be home in a couple of hours. I'll give her a call."

"Okay, the last three officers that were briefed before the Chinese reacted were Handy, Farrell and Kelly. If the leaker isn't Handy, does that mean it has to be Farrell or Kelly?'

"One would think, but when we met with them, we thought they were clean."

CHAPTER 23

Cory agreed to come up to the city after work on Friday evening. Cal joined them at Jonathan's home. After they settled in, Cal said, "I agree we're going to keep pursuing the leak, but I don't know where to start."

Cory was uneasy. "Now that we're not working with the DIA, Lockheed won't be agreeing to have me take time off like before."

Jonathan had remained silent as his friends expressed their concerns. He looked up and said, "Perhaps we need fresh eyes."

Cory and Cal stared at him, waiting for him to flush out his thoughts. "Why don't we bring in the Pacific Avenue Irregulars?"

The Pacific Avenue Irregulars were a collection of Jonathan and Cal's friends. They originally met monthly to play poker at Cal's condo, but had come to Jonathan's aid when he became a person of interest in what came to be called The Culprit Murders. The group's three dominant characteristics were beyond Mensa in brilliant minds, unquestioned loyalty to their friends, and zero skill at playing poker. Carlos Hermosillo, a renowned physicist at Stanford, had named the group, lifting the name of the street urchins utilized by Sherlock Holmes.

Cal thought for a moment. "I know they weren't interested in getting involved with our last investigation, but I'm sure they'll jump at this."

Cory seemed doubtful. "Do you think they can help?"

Jonathan smiled, "I don't know, but they're all above genius level. Let's give it a try."

Cal gave the idea enthusiastic approval. "I'll make the calls right now. If they're available, how about tomorrow at my place?"

Jonathan nodded. "Tomorrow's fine, but let's meet here. Parking will be a lot easier and, while your place might not be bugged, we know mine is clean."

Cal began making the calls on his cell. When he stressed the importance of the meeting, all four men agreed to come.

The meeting had been set for seven o'clock and everyone arrived on time. Alan Thielen and Harold Kurtovich, both working on advanced weapons design at Lockheed actually arrived fifteen minutes early. Carlos was next, followed by Greg Stokes, who headed the biotech research department at Genentech. They all appeared curious and somewhat enthused about Cal's cryptic phone call. This was also the first time they had been to Jonathan's new home and they were obviously impressed. Carlos and Greg, who had not previously met Cory, were also impressed by the beautiful woman.

Once everyone was seated in the living room, Cal stood up and gave a brief history of their involvement with the Defense Intelligence Agency and their efforts to find the person leaking secrets to the Chinese.

At one point, Jonathan described the plan to locate the traitor through the false briefing and the DIA's conclusion that Colonel Rayman Hardy was the leaker. He went on to explain why they believed Hardy was not the leaker.

When Cal and Jonathan were finished, there was a moment of silence as the four men absorbed what they had just heard. Greg Stokes was the first to speak. "I assume the DIA has a lot of really bright people. Can't they see what you see?"

Jonathan fielded the question. "I'm sure you're right. They have a lot of smart people, but they were under enormous pressure, and they're bureaucrats. The guy who led our little efforts needed a quick win."

Cal said, "Help us figure out a plan. The nine people we investigated all seemed clean. We're trying to figure out what to do next."

Carlos stood up. "I don't think that this is something we can come up with in the next ten minutes. Why don't we all think about it and meet again in a few days?"

Jonathan glanced at the four men. "But you all agree to help us?"

All four men nodded. A few minutes later, they were headed home.

———

The two men in the car a few houses away watched the men leave. One picked up his phone and described the meeting. He read off the license plates of the departing cars before settling in to wait for the team that would replace them.

Their controller had no idea what to make of the information. He immediately called his contact and instructed the man to identify the owners of the departed vehicles. Within twenty minutes he had the information and relayed it to Bejing.

CHAPTER 24

After his coffee, juice, and *Chronicle* routine, Jonathan turned on Fox to catch up on the national news. A reporter was interviewing a Republican congressman outside the Capitol building when the interview was interrupted by breaking news. A breathless morning host announced the arrest of a full bird colonel at the Pentagon. While no official information had been released, sources revealed the man was being charged with espionage.

Jonathan was not shocked by the story; he was convinced that Handy's arrest was a mistake. A few hours later, Cal called.

Cal's voice was shaking when he said, "Woodward called. He thinks we leaked the story. He was over the top over-the-top, irate, and quoted a bunch of statutes that he said we violated. He said he was going to send us to Guantanamo."

"Of course, you denied being the source."

"Yeah, but he wasn't buying it. He hinted that if Cory and I cooperated, he would only go after you."

"I guess my close relationship with him has gone south."

"Pardon me if I'm not laughing."

"This is crazy. How can they have a case if we didn't talk to the press? Cal, are you on your cell or your landline?"

There was a pause. "Landline."

"Hang up. I'll call you on your cell."

A moment later, Cal answered on his cell. "Sorry, I'm a little shook up. I don't think we said anything that could hurt us, and I don't think my landline has been compromised."

"No, we didn't. Assuming everything is still classified, our only problem would be sharing the information with Myron and the Irregulars."

Late in the afternoon, Jonathan's doorbell rang. Before opening the door, he looked at the screen from his security system. Two Caucasian men in suits were standing on his landing. When he opened the door, one man produced his badge.

"Homeland Security, are you Jonathan Scanlan?"

"Yes."

"You need to come with us.'"

Bo was standing next to Jonathan. "I need to call someone to come and take care of my dog."

The man who had produced his badge grabbed Jonathan, which made Bo show his teeth and offer a deep growl. The man released Jonathan and began to draw his gun.

His partner shouted, "Sam, back off." Everyone stood still for a moment. The second man said, "Go ahead. Call someone to take care of the dog. We'll be monitoring the call, so don't try something stupid."

He debated for a moment between Cory and Cal, quickly deciding on Cory. When she picked up, he said, "I'm being taken in by Homeland Security, please get back here and take care of Bo."

When he hung up, he was handcuffed and hustled to a Crown Vic. He was shoved into the back without comment and driven to the Phillip Burton Federal Building on Golden Gate Avenue. No one spoke during the ride.

He was marched into the building, eventually landing in an interrogation room on the second floor. Still cuffed, he was left to marinate for over an hour before a man entered the room. He was in his midfifties, with grey hair cut short and a complexion paler than a new moon. He wore wire-rimmed glasses and a neutral expression.

"My name is Garland Lombardi. I'm the head of our San Francisco office. Let me get you out of those cuffs."

Jonatha said nothing. Lombardi continued. "Do you know why you're here?"

"No."

"We have sources that indicate you provided classified government information to the media. What do you have to say about that?"

"Not true."

"Look, perhaps you didn't know what you passed on was classified. You have a clean record. I'm sure we can work something out."

"I've had no contact with the media, so your sources are mistaken, and I want to contact my lawyer."

Lombardi stared at Jonathan for several minutes without speaking, hoping the uncomfortable silence would bring about more comments. It did not.

The Homeland man sighed and sat down. "So, you're an innocent man."

"Yes, and I'm quite sure your *source* is a man named Forrest Woodward at the Defense Intelligence Agency."

This seemed to take Garland Lombardi by surprise. "Why would this man be our source?"

"Two friends of mine, Cory Bishop, Cal Hulse, and I were brought in by the DIA and Woodward to root out whoever has been leaking information at the Pentagon. Woodward and I dislike each other, and I believe it's become personal."

Lombardi sat back and thought for a moment. "So, if you didn't contact the media, who did?"

"Who knows. There are about twenty-three thousand people working at the Pentagon."

"I don't know. It seems unrealistic that this man, Woodward, would go that far."

"Check out what evidence they have that I contacted the media; there won't be any. Besides, I don't believe the man they arrested, Colonel Raymond Handy, leaked the information to the Chinese."

Garland Lombardi stood up and left the room without speaking. An hour later, he returned, shook his head, and said, "Let me get someone to drive you home."

As he was leaving, Jonathan paused. "Any relation to Vince Lombardi?"

The Homeland man smiled. "I wish."

When Jonathan reached home, he found Cory sitting with Bo.

Cory was obviously shaken. "I came up, but I didn't know what I could do."

"They took me in, believing I had placed the story about Handy with the media. I'm pretty sure Woodward sicced them on me."

Cory shook her head. "You've been picked up by the police, the FBI, and now Homeland. What's next, the Coast Guard?"

CHAPTER 25

It was the middle of the night in Beijing, but a hasty meeting had been organized. Dong Jun turned to the head of Intelligence. "What do you make of this meeting and these people?"

"I'm not sure, but the meeting was quite short, so not a social gathering. I'll have more information on the four men later in the day."

Jun shook his head. "The only reason Hulse, Scanlan and Bishop would have organized such a meeting is to continue the investigation."

"The Woodward man was not present."

"So, like the Independence investigation, they're doing this on their own?"

"That would appear to be the case. Do you want to eliminate them?"

"Probably, but let's first find out more about the men they met with."

Three hours later, the Minister of Defense and head of Intelligence met in the conference room next to Jun's office. This time, several aides were called in.

Jun stared impatiently at Chan Wening. "What do you have?"

Wening turned and nodded to one of his aides. The man stepped forward. "Sir, the men are Greg Stokes, Carlos Hermosillo, Alan Thielen, and Harold Kurtovich. Stokes is a research biologist, Hermosillo is a physicist, Thielen and Kurtovich are advanced weapon design experts."

Jun sat back in his chair, clearly puzzled. "None of these people are investigators."

Wening pointed to another of his aides. The aide stepped forward. "Sir, I was tasked to read the three books written by Jonathan Scanlan. In the second book, *The Culprit Murders*, a group of Scanlan's friends assisted him. The individuals are not identified."

Jun offered a grim smile. "So, they are an informal think tank."

Wening nodded. "That is what we think."

Jun took a moment before turning to Wening. "They may be highly intelligent, but can they help with the investigation?"

The head of Intelligence leaned forward, his eyes intense. "If we eliminate Scanlan, Hulse and the woman, it would not matter if these people can help."

"Yes, arrange for it to happen."

When Wening began to stand, the minister waved him back to his chair. "There would be an international incident if Chinese operatives killed the three people that were investigating the information being leaked to us. Use the cartels."

"The cartels? Can we order them to do this?"

"They will if they wish to keep receiving our fentanyl."

CHAPTER 26

Jonathan looked out his kitchen window at the gathering clouds. Rain was forecast for later in the day. He glanced at Bo. "All right, big boy. Let me change, and we'll go for a run before it starts coming down." At the word, run, Bo began spinning around in anticipation.

As he left the house and began crossing the street with Bo on his leash, he saw two men step out of their car, which was parked across from his neighbor's house. Both men were staring at him as they moved toward Jonathan. Jonathan could see guns in their hands.

Jonathan's mind raced. He was too far from his house to make it home. He sprinted into the Presidio. The first shot hit a tree next to him as he entered the park. He and Bo ran as fast as they could down a path that led away from the street.

The men ran into the park, firing at Jonathan. Firing while running proved difficult as the shots went wide of their target. Also, the narrowness of the footpath meant Jonathan's pursuers were forced to run in single file, and neither man was wearing running shoes, which allowed Jonathan to gain a great deal of separation quickly. Jonathan did not stop and look back until he was sure the men had turned back.

While he was in great shape, his chest was heaving, and he was sweating heavily from fear and his all-out sprint. Bo seemed unaffected by their morning dash and appeared disappointed when Jonathan finally turned back toward his home.

He paused before exiting the Presidio and looked down the street. The men and their car were gone. Once he and Bo were safely in their home, he thought about who to call. His first thought was to call the police. While that would be the normal reaction, he knew that would yield nothing. He believed the men were Hispanic, but he could not describe them in any detail. Their car was a beige sedan, but he could not identify the make. Instead, he called Cal.

As usual, it went to voicemail. He shouted into the phone, "Call me. It's urgent!"

A half hour later, Cal called. "What happened?"

Jonathan again shouted into his phone. "Two guys just tried to kill me."

There was a moment of silence and Jonathan thought he had lost the connection. Then Cal said, "Holy shit. Have you called the police?"

Jonathan had calmed down enough to lower his voice. "I thought about it, but I didn't see the two guys that shot at me well enough to describe them or pick them out of a lineup."

"They shot at you?"

"Yeah, Bo and I were going to go for a run. They began shooting at us as we were about to enter the Presidio. They chased us, but we were able to get away."

"Didn't somebody hear the shots and call the police?"

"The shots weren't that loud, I guess they were using silencers."

"What are you going to do?"

Jonathan thought for a moment. "Call Myron."

"Okay. Do you think it's because we're looking for the leaker?"

It was Jonathan's turn to pause. "Probably, or maybe exposing Independence. I think the men were Hispanic."

"Really, Hispanic. I would have guessed Chinese."

"Maybe just thugs for hire."

"I guess Cory and I need to watch what we're doing."

Jonathan's thinking had not gotten that far. "Absolutely. I'm not looking forward to telling her that we're back in the frying pan."

Jonathan's next call was to Myron Rossi. When Myron picked up, he said, "Rossi Investigative Services."

"Myron, it's Jonathan. My situation has heated up. Two guys just tried to shoot me."

"I'll be there tomorrow. Are the police involved?"

"No. I didn't see the point. I didn't see them well enough to identify them."

"Okay, stay inside until I get there. Are Cory and Cal in danger?"

"Probably."

"I may need to line up a couple of guys to help cover them."

"Whatever you think you need."

Jonathan was dreading his next call. When Cory did not answer, he left a message asking for a call back."

When Cory called, her voice was upbeat. "Hi, just got back from shopping. What's happening?"

Jonathan needed to warn Cory, but he did not want to throw her into a panic. "Well, you know I've had a couple of guys watching my house. I think things have escalated. I noticed they were armed. I called Myron, and he'll be here tomorrow. I just wanted to warn you."

"Oh no, is this Independence all over again?" Jonathan could hear the fear in her voice.

"I hope not. Do you think Woodward could have his people protect us?"

Cory thought for a moment. "I don't know. I can call him."

Jonathan thought it would not help the man's career if the people he brought in to find the leaker got whacked, but on the other hand, the man was a colossal asshole. "Give him a call."

Later that evening, Cory called. "I don't think Woodward is going to help. He hemmed and hawed and finally said that the DIA doesn't have resources for that kind of work."

"I'm not surprised."

"Well, we have Myron."

"He said he might be bringing in a couple of his friends."

"You think Cal and I might also be in danger?"

"I don't know, but like the Boy Scout motto, be prepared."

CHAPTER 27

Jonathan's narrow escape did not sit well in Beijing. Dong Jun, wearing his usual Mao garb, looked across his desk at Chan Wening. The younger man appeared unfazed by the failed attempt. Unlike the minister, Wening wore stylish Western clothes

"This bungled attempt will put Scanlan and the others on guard."

"True, but we've seen no sign that the Defense Intelligence Agency, or any other government agency, is providing protection."

"The attempt was quite crude."

"The cartels are not known for their sophistication, but they have unlimited manpower, and they can be very effective."

Jun gave Wening a hard look. "It should not be a difficult task to eliminate these three people. We cannot lose our man in Washington."

Chan Wening was not a man to be easily rattled, but his body tensed at the implied threat. While the plump man across from him in his Mao suit looked like everybody's favorite grandfather, he knew the minister to be without mercy when failure occurred.

"It will happen. Perhaps I should be there to ensure success."

"Yes, perhaps you should."

———

Carlos Hermosillo called Cal and left a message, asking him to return his call as soon as possible. An hour later, his phone rang.

"Hi, Carlos, did the Irregulars come up with anything?"

"Maybe, we need to get together. How about seven on Friday at your place?"

"Fine, Myron will be joining us."

Jonathan, Cory, and Myron arrived early. Cal offered coffee, and they all sat around, waiting for the others to arrive. Cal turned to Jonathan. "Myron checked out the condo. No bugs."

Jonathan nodded but remained silent. Alan, Harold, and Carlos arrived on time. When Greg Stokes arrived fifteen minutes later, he began bitching about the lack of parking around the condominium.

Carlos stood up and motioned for the chattering to stop. "All right. We've spent some time throwing around ideas and, while we have no idea who the leaker is, we do have some thoughts. Your fake briefing narrowed it down to three Pentagon people, and you don't believe the man the DIA has taken into custody is guilty, and you believe the other two are also innocent. Greg had some questions that we believe make sense. Apparently, the three people who received the false briefing, which the Chinese reacted to, were senior officers, generals, and colonels. Wouldn't other lower-level people be involved, you know, preparing the briefings, making copies, stuff like that?"

Cal, Cory, and Jonathan glanced at each other. After a moment, Jonathan said, "I'm sure you're right. The information in the briefings is highly classified, so the number would be small."

Cal looked embarrassed. "I can't believe we didn't see that."

Jonathan smiled and said, "This is great. Now we're talking about the support staff for the two generals and the colonel, so we need to look at several people, but this is something we can work on."

After a long round of self-congratulations, the Irregulars left for home. Cal, Cory, Myron, and Jonathan huddled when they were alone. Cory brought up the obvious obstacle. "I don't think Woodward will give us the names of the support people. He's banking on Handy."

Jonathan looked at Cal, who shook his head. "No way can I hack the Pentagon's systems."

No conclusion was reached as the three left Cal's condo. Myron was aware of a dark colored SUV that followed.

When they reached Jonathan's home, Myron noticed that Jonathan had locked the entry door, but had not set the alarm.

"Jonathan, set the alarm."

Jonathan gave the big man a puzzled look. "But we're inside. I only set the alarm when we go out."

Myron shook his head. "You have to get in the habit of using the alarm, whether you're in the house or out. Remember what happened in Cupertino?"

It took a moment for Myron's comment to register. A woman had been able to enter the house they were renting in the middle of the night. "You're right." He went back to the panel and activated the system.

Myron turned to Cory. "The man who'll be with you when you're not here is named Jim Stack, but everyone calls him JS."

"You really think this is necessary?"

Myron nodded. "They tried to take out Jonathan, so there's no reason they wouldn't also go after you and Cal."

Cory stood up and gasped as she stared at Jonathan. "What do you mean, they tried to take Jonathan out?"

Ah, shit was the thought that went through Jonathan's mind.

Myron realized Jonathan had not told Cory everything. His face flushed as he mumbled, "I think I'll have a beer." He moved quickly into the kitchen.

"JONATHAN!"

Jonathan was equally embarrassed. "Look, I didn't want to upset you. Everything's okay, I'm fine."

Tears were steaming down Cory's face. It took her several minutes to control herself. "Jonathan, I love you. You can't lie to me."

Jonathan was about to say he did not lie; he just did not tell her everything. Realizing such a comment would not help his cause, he went to her, embraced her, and whispered, "I'm sorry. I won't do that again."

Cory gradually calmed. "You have to always tell me the truth." Jonathan simply nodded.

CHAPTER 28

Jonathan, Cal, and Cory met the following day at Cal's condo. Myron's man, Lamar Williams, a six-foot-three muscular black man with a shaved Michael Jordan dome, sat in the kitchen drinking coffee.

"Okay, looking at Handy, Farrell and Kelly's aides is a great idea, but the Pentagon isn't about to give us an organization chart."

Jonathan nodded in agreement. "And we're not about to get any help from Woodward. We have friendlies at the FBI, with Carmen and Cain, but they wouldn't have access."

Cory glanced at her friends. "I know Handy is out of reach, but do you think Kelly and Farrell might help us?"

Jonathan shook his head. "After Handy's arrest and the heat that had to follow, I'm sure they wouldn't open their doors."

Cal said, "Don't look at me. I'd spend the rest of my life in Leavenworth if I tried to hack their systems."

Without anyone having a brilliant idea, the brief gathering broke up. When Cory and Jonathan left the building, Myron was waiting in his Lincoln.

When Jonathan slid into the passenger seat, he turned to Myron. "Anyone watching us?"

"I think so. There's a silver Ford SUV down the street. We'll see if they follow up at home."

When Myron pulled away from the curb, the silver Ford followed, staying well back.

Days later, Jonathan tossed and turned in bed, his mind cluttered with unanswered questions. The frustration of having a path forward but having no ability to pursue their inquiries was driving him up the wall. Dawn was breaking when Jonathan sat upright in bed as a thought came to him. No solution, but a possible way forward.

He leaped out of bed and stumbled into the bathroom. He splashed water on his face, trying to clear his mind. Bo moved out of his dog bed and sat anxiously staring at his master. Jonathan threw on jeans and a sweatshirt, went to the kitchen, and turned on his coffee maker. He filled a mug and sat at his kitchen table, trying to flesh out his thoughts. He wanted to call Cory, but knew it was way too early.

Jonathan's activities brought Myron into the room. He filled his cup and joined Jonathan at the table. He gave a questioning look across the table but said nothing.

"I have an idea which might let us move forward."

"Care to share?"

"When Homeland dragged me downtown, I was questioned by the head of the San Francisco office, a man named Garland Lonbardi."

Myron waited for the rest. "He's a smart guy, and he quickly figured out the charges were bogus. He might be in a position to help us."

"Even if he could help you, would he?"

"I don't know, but I have to give it a try. He's all I've got."

Later that morning, he called Cory when he thought he could catch her before she went to work. When she answered, Jonathan told her his idea.

"Do you think he'll help us?" She sounded doubtful.

"He may not be able to get us what we need and, even if he could, he may not be willing to do so, but we have to try."

"Look, I have to go. Call me after you talk to him. Good luck."

Jonathan spent the next two hours trying to develop a compelling argument that would convince Garland Lombardi to work with his team of three. A few thoughts came to mind, but he had little confidence that his effort would be successful.

He googled the telephone number for the San Francisco Homeland Security office. A woman answered.

"Homeland Security, how can I help you?"

"I would like to speak with Garland Lombardi."

"May I ask what this is regarding?"

The gatekeeper. "I'm sorry, but no. Please tell him my name, Jonathan Scanlan."

"I'm sorry, but I would need to know what this is regarding."

"Tell Garland, security leaks at the Pentagon."

There was a pause before she said, "Just a moment, please."

After several minutes, Garland Lombardi came on the line. "Mr. Scanlan, how can I help you?"

"As I mentioned at our meeting, we're trying to identify the person leaking sensitive information to one of our adversaries. I would like to meet with you to see if you could help us."

"I don't see how I can contribute anything."

"I'm not sure you can, but I'll only take up no more than twenty minutes of your time."

After a long pause, Lombardi said, "All right. My office tomorrow morning at ten."

"Thank you, I'll be there."

Jonathan knew Woodward would do everything he could to destroy him if he learned of the meeting, but if you could not discuss national security with Homeland Security, who would you talk to?

Cal called later, and Jonathan described his conversation with Lombardi. When he finished, Cal sounded less than convinced. "You think he can help us?"

"I don't know, but I think it's worth a try. You want to come with me?"

Cal hesitated. "No. I think you're better off solo on this one. And if he contacts Woodward, you'll need someone to post your bail."

"Very funny."

"Not so funny."

Jonathan worked on what he planned to tell Lombardi, made a few notes, and placed them in a briefcase he had hardly ever used.

CHAPTER 29

Jonathan felt like he was about to dive off the high board at the Fleishhacker pool as he walked into the Homeland office ten minutes early. He gave the receptionist his name and took a seat in the waiting area.

Garland Lombardi walked in from one of the outer offices, smiled, and offered Jonathan his hand. After the cordial greeting, Jonathan followed the man down a corridor and into Lombardi's private office. Jonathan glanced around, noting the man did not have the usual vanity wall with an array of pictures showing himself with various notable people.

Lombardi motioned Jonathan toward the visitor's chairs. He sat, nervously cleared his throat, and said, "Thank you for seeing me."

Lombardi did not respond as he studied Jonathan with curiosity.

"As I said, three of us were tasked by DIA with trying to locate the person leaking information at the Pentagon. The agency believes they've located the leaker, Colonel Raymon Hardy. We believe Hardy was set up. They said classified information was on his home computer, but the time stamp on the entry doesn't make sense. We believe the leak is coming from a mole on the staff of one of three officers, Colonel Handy, General Michael Kelly or General James Farrell."

"You've expressed your belief to DIA?"

"Yes, and they were not interested. They believe they have the leaker."

"Have you met this man, Colonel Handy?"

"Yes, we interviewed him."

"What was your impression?"

"He's an arrogant asshole, but we believe he's an innocent arrogant asshole."

Jonathan's comment seemed to amuse Lombardi. "So… why are you here?"

"I'm here because I have nowhere else to go. When we met, I thought you were intelligent and dedicated to doing the right thing. We're trying to obtain the names of the staff support people serving the three officers I mentioned."

After a long pause, Lombardi shook his head. "I'm sorry, but I can't help you."

Jonathan nodded and reached into his briefcase. "These are the names and contact numbers of two people at the local FBI office. If you wish to check me out, talk to them. I assure you I'm not some conspiracy nut. Thank you again for your time."

Jonathan stood up and walked out of Garland Lombardi's office.

Jonathan checked his messages when he reached home. Both Cal and Cory had called, asking for an update. When he called Cal, he was surprised when his friend picked up, rather than having the call go to voicemail.

"How did it go?"

"The meeting was cordial. He listened to me, asked a few questions, and told me he couldn't help us."

"Well, it was worth a try. I don't see how we can move forward."

"Unfortunately, I'm afraid you're right."

"Dinner tonight?"

"Not tonight. I'll call you later in the week."

Virtually the same conversation occurred when he talked to Cory.

He was mopping around the house when Myron joined him. "The plan didn't work?"

Jonathan did not bother to reply. "You know, right now I'd really like to go for a run to clear my mind, but I don't want to get shot at."

After a brief hesitation, Myron said, "Look, I'll go out and see if they're out there."

The big man walked out of the house and checked the street in both directions. A black sedan was parked three houses down on the Presidio side of the street. He could see two figures inside the car. He drew his Glock, keeping it down by his side as he walked toward the vehicle. When he was ten yards away, the car started and screeched away from the curb.

Myron studied the two men in the car as it passed him and disappeared down the street. He returned to the house and smiled at Jonathan. "You can go for your run."

"No one was out there?"

"Two Hispanic guys were there, but they left."

Jonathan gave Myron a questioning look, then went to his room to change.

Two days later, Jonathan's phone chirped with a call from an unfamiliar number. He picked up and was surprised to hear Garland Lombardi's voice.

"Good morning, Jonathan, would you be free to meet today?"

Jonathan was momentarily stunned and took a moment to reply. "Of course."

"There's a diner named Half Day Café two blocks from my office. One o'clock?"

"Sure."

Jonathan had no idea what had changed, but it could only be for the better. He googled the café, writing down the address. When the meeting time was approaching, he had Myron drive him to the café. He arrived fifteen minutes early. Myron waited in the Lincoln. Jonathan was able to secure a booth with a view of the café's front door. He ordered coffee and watched as the lunch crowd began to thin out.

The head of the Homeland office came in, spotted Jonathan, and slid into the booth. He laid a folder on the table. He ordered coffee with cream and did not speak until the coffee arrived and the waitress had moved away.

His expression was as grim as a heart attack. "I checked you out with your FBI contacts and some other sources. I have to say I'm impressed. The Independence exposure was great work. I also gave your request a good deal of thought. If this man, Handy, is not leaking our plans, I want the leaker caught and the leaks stopped. Before moving to Homeland, I was an officer in the Army, and I still have high-level contacts. What I'm about to give you did not come from me, you understand?"

When Jonathan nodded, Lombardi pushed the file folder across the table, stood up and left the café. Jonathan did not open the folder. He put twenty dollars on the table, left the restaurant and walked down the street, and slid into the Lincoln.

When he was back in his house, he began reviewing the information. It included the names of the aides and other support people for the three men. He called Cal and left an urgent message to return his call. He decided to wait and call Cory when she was home from work.

Ten minutes later, Cal called. "What's so urgent?"

"Lombardi came through. I have the names of Handy, Farrell, and Kelly's support people."

"Holy shit. How did that happen?"

"The man decided to do the right thing. By the way, we don't know anyone named Lombardi."

"I understand. Bring me the names so I can start digging."

"I'll send Myron. I don't want to be meeting our 'friends'."

"Fine."

Cal called several hours after Myron had returned. "Hi Jon. This is going to take a while. Each of the men has a pretty healthy number of supporting staff. The total is sixteen, and all we have is their rank, if they're military, and which officer they report to."

"What do you think we should be looking for?"

There was a pause. "I'm not sure. I'll look for money, but that may not be the motivator in this case, and, even if it is, it would probably be well hidden."

"I have to hope that by looking into their backgrounds, something will stand out."

"Maybe." Cal did not sound optimistic.

"If we can narrow it down, like we did with the officers, Cory and I could go back to DC."

"Remember, Cory isn't willing to leave her job over this, and Woodward isn't about to pull any strings at Lockheed."

"You're right. Well, do your best and let's see where we are."

Cory called later that evening. "Evening, professor. Did Cal have any ideas when he got the list?"

"No. He's going to dig in, but he's not sure what he should be looking for, besides money."

Cory thought for a moment. "I can see the problem. If it's money, the Chinese aren't going to be filling up the leaker's checking account, and we can assume the person isn't stupid enough to be purchasing expensive toys."

"And it may not be money."

"I can see that ferreting out the mole is going to be a problem. Hey, ever since you were shot at, we've been acting like shut-ins. Any chance we can do something fun on the weekend?"

"You're right. Anything in mind?"

"Not off the top. It would be great to get out of town."

"Let's see what we can come up with. I'll call you tomorrow."

CHAPTER 30

Jonathan gave Cory a call, catching her before she left for work. "Hi, do you have any vacation time left?"

"Sure, quite a bit. What are you thinking about?"

"Hawaii. Have you been there?"

"A few years ago, a girlfriend and I went to Maui for a week."

"How about the Big Island? I'll book a week at one of the resorts. I thought about going somewhere close to home, but with the bad guys hanging around, Hawaii seemed like a better choice."

"I'll start packing my bikini. When do you want to leave?"

"Let's leave Saturday and come back next Saturday."

"Let me clear it at work, but I'm sure there won't be a problem. What about Bo?"

"Myron will stay at the house and take care of him."

"This is going to be fun."

Three days later, Jonathan met Cory at the airport. They ordered coffee as they waited for their flight in the United wing of the terminal. Jonathan was happy to see Cory taking her Zoloft before boarding.

Cory dozed while Jonathan read *Shaken,* John Gresham's newest book. Cory was starting to come around as they made their descent. As first-class passengers with only carry-on bags, they were able to walk through the terminal and directly to a cab stand.

Once on the road, Cory was startled by the passing landscape. "This looks like we landed on the moon."

"It's all lava from the island's volcano, which is still quite active. They have helicopter tours that take tourists right over it, but I didn't think that was something you'd want to do."

Cory gave him a weak smile. "Thank you. Is the resort we're going to like this?" She waved at the lava-covered hillside.

He smiled and took her hand. "No, it's very lush and tropical."

Eventually, the cab turned off the highway onto a road leading toward the ocean. They passed a modestly sized mall and finally stopped in front of the Mauna Kea Beach Hotel. The driver took their bags from the trunk and handed them to a waiting bellhop.

Fifteen minutes later they were in their suite admiring the ocean view. An attractive basket of fruit was on one of the tables.

"Jonathan, this is wonderful."

Jonathan smiled, enjoying Cory's reaction. "What do you feel like doing?"

"Well, for starters, let's get something to eat."

Jonathan, who had been served on the plane, realized Cory's last meal was probably last night's dinner. "Sure, let's go downstairs."

Having arrived after the lunch rush, they were seated at a table with an expansive view of the ocean and lagoon. Jonathan, who was not that hungry, ordered two appetizers and a beer, while Cory went with a seafood platter and a glass of Chardonnay.

The week passed at a leisurely pace. In the morning, Jonathan would go for a run, followed by time with Cory at the resort's pool. One day, they rented a car for a drive along the island's western coast, including a stop at the Parker Ranch.

Some evenings were spent at one of the hotel's restaurants, but for a change of pace, they dined at the Seafood Bar & Grill, the Napua at the Mauna Lani Beach Club, and the nearby Tommy Bahama restaurant.

At dinner, on their last evening at the resort, Cory looked across the table at Jonathan and smiled. "This has been wonderful. My only problem is that I'll have to diet like crazy when we get back. I love this place."

"You know, we could always buy a place over here."

"Maybe someday, but remember I'm still a working girl with only so much vacation time."

The balance of the evening was spent trying to work off the island's excellent cuisine in the bedroom.

———

Minister Dong Jun knew that Jonathan Scanlan and Cory Bishop were out of reach while they were in Hawaii, but that did not lessen his impatience. Chan Wening had made his way to San Francisco to supervise the hits on Jonathan and his friends. He, too, was impatient and also annoyed by the minister's daily calls, as there was nothing to report. Given where Cal Hulse lived, only light surveillance was possible, and there had been no opportunity to take the man out. He was also less than impressed by the quality of the cartel personnel that had been given the task. While they were experienced killers, they were simply brutal thugs and, in his opinion, not terribly bright.

Perhaps as a result of his society's ingrained sexist culture, he placed more importance on eliminating Hulse and Scanlan than he did on the woman.

He had been briefed on Scanlan and Bishop's airline reservations and was considering having them hit as soon as they arrived. Airport security eliminated the possibility of taking action inside the terminal, but perhaps they could be killed as they waited for their ride. The idea lifted his spirits.

CHAPTER 31

Chan Wening glanced around the living room of the rental he had acquired in the city's Outer Mission District. The five men that the Sinaloa cartel had provided ranged in age from twenty to forty. Only two spoke English fluently.

Wening described the hit as he distributed photos of Jonathan Scanlan to each of the men. He waited for one of the English speakers to translate that this was the primary target. He told them that Scanlan would be with an attractive blond-haired woman, but that he had no photo of the woman. She was also to be killed.

After translating this information, the translator asked if either person would be armed. Wening shook his head. When this was translated, the cartel men laughed.

The reaction irritated Wening. He did not mention the Independence debacle, but warned them that earlier attempts on the man had failed.

One of the men laughed and said something to the translator, who smiled and said, "What will this man do, hide behind the woman?"

Wening offered a grim smile. He told them the plane's arrival time and that the man and woman would be leaving the United domestic terminal on the arrival level. He added that he would have a spotter inside the terminal who would follow the couple and let them know when they passed through the secure area. He passed out earbuds that would allow him to communicate with them during the hit.

While the hit was simple enough, Wening felt the men were barely paying attention. If these were his men, such an attitude would not be tolerated. He then took the two English speakers and drove them to the airport. When they reached the United terminal, he pulled to the curb and pointed out where Scanlan and Bishop would be exiting the building. He pointed out the congestion, as cars were arriving to pick up and drop off passengers.

The two men nodded and pointed to a uniformed policeman who seemed to be there to keep traffic moving. Wening thought a rapid exit after the shooting would be difficult, but did not express his thoughts. He really did not care if the cartel men would be able to escape.

———

Jonathan and Cory followed what had become their normal routine. When they arrived at the Ellison Onizuka International Airport, they checked in and received their boarding passes. Just before boarding, Cory took her pills. Once settled in their seats on the plane, Jonathan watched as the Zoloft began to have the desired effect. He pulled Patterson's latest book from his bag and made himself comfortable. When they landed, Jonathan helped Cory out of her seat and off the plane. The effect of the antianxiety pills was wearing off, but she still needed assistance. When they were in the terminal, Jonathan led her to a vacant chair. He called Myron, told him that they had landed and that Cory needed time for the Zoloft to wear off.

Myron, who was on his way to pick them up, agreed to kill time until Jonathan could get her outside. Jonathan went to one of the concessions and purchased a cup of coffee. The coffee had the desired effect, allowing Cory to weakly walk, with Jonathan's assistance.

When they were halfway to the exit, he called Myron with an update. By the time they walked past the baggage area, Myron was waiting with the Lincoln. One of the cartel shooters was waiting outside the terminal on the sidewalk. The uniformed policeman saw the man as he raised his gun and realized what was happening.

He pulled his service weapon and yelled at the man to drop his gun. When the shooter spun around and aimed at the cop, the policeman killed him with two quick shots.

Myron had stepped out of his car with his weapon drawn. Jonathan pulled Cory to the ground by the side of the Lincoln as two other men stepped out of a car that had been double-parked twenty yards away. They had no clear shot at Jonathan, so they quickly moved toward the sidewalk. One of the men took a shot at Myron, missing him and shattering the windshield of a nearby car.

Myron calmly shot the man trying to move around the cover of the Lincoln. The second man took another shot at Myron, which went wide, hitting a nearby woman in the shoulder. Myron's second shot dropped the man, hitting him in the forehead.

The policeman was yelling for everyone to drop their weapons. He did not fire again as he was unsure who he should be firing at.

Wening, in a car with one of the English speakers, screamed for the remaining man to leave. In history's slowest exit from a shootout, he and the English speaker slowly merged into traffic and drove away. The remaining cartel man in a second car wormed his way through the congested traffic and out of the airport.

Myron laid his Glock on the hood of the Lincoln Continental and helped Jonathan and Cory to their feet. Jonathan patted the big man on his shoulder, and said, "Take care of Cory." He then went to the woman, who was on the ground crying and gripping her shoulder. The policeman pushed him aside and began applying pressure to the wound.

Within minutes, an ambulance arrived, followed by several black and whites. The woman was quickly attended to, placed on a gurney, and driven away with lights and sirens. The police told Myron, Jonathan, and Cory to wait for the detectives to arrive.

Two detectives, who identified themselves as Louis Tosse and Audrey Sartorio, pulled up in an unmarked. They told one of the uniforms to stay with Cory while they separated Myron and Jonathan.

Each detective took one of the men and placed them in the backseat of a patrol car, leaving the door open as they asked their questions.

"Your name, please."

"Jonathan Scanlan."

"Why were you at the airport?"

"Cory Bishop, the woman in the Lincoln, and I just arrived from Hawaii."

"Who are the men who just tried to shoot you?"

"I have no idea. I've never seen them before."

Detective Tosse gave Jonathan a look of total disbelief. "Come on now. Why were they trying to kill you?"

"Again, no idea."

"You'll have to do better than that. I understand the big man over there is a private detective. Why do you need a private detective?"

"Myron is a friend of mine. He's staying at my house in the city and offered to pick us up."

A clearly frustrated detective shook his head. "You'll have to do better than that."

Jonathan gave the man a cold stare. "No, I don't."

"I can haul your ass in."

"Yes, and I can call my lawyer. Maybe you're familiar with her, Costantine Welland?"

The attorney's name had the desired effect. "She's your lawyer?"

"Yes, do I need to give her a call?"

"Stay right here."

Tosse went over to the other patrol car, where Detective Sartorio was questioning Myron. Tosse turned to his partner. "Anything?"

"No. He says he was just here to pick up his friends."

"What about the woman?"

"I wouldn't go there. She's really shook up."

"Let me see what the brass has to say." He moved away and called Lincoln Fenton, the head of the city's detectives. He described what he knew of the situation and summarized Rossi and Scanlan's statements.

After a good deal of back-and-forth, Tosse was told to schedule a time for the three to come in to make a formal statement.

Reluctantly, Myron, Cory, and Jonathan were released. Myron was unhappy that his Glock was taken by the police.

CHAPTER 32

Chan Wening was speechless. The bungled attempt on Scanlan and Bishop was beyond incompetence. He knew the congested airport situation created problems, but the inability of three shooters to kill an unarmed man and woman was absurd.

When he was back in his hotel room, he used his encrypted phone to reach the Minister of National Defense. The time difference between San Francisco and Beijing was sixteen hours. He tried to calm himself before he recorded his message.

"The cartel men are incompetent. They blew the attempt on Scanlan and the woman. I need the best assassin we have. Three cartel men are dead, and I instructed the other two to leave the country. While this is a mess, our involvement is not known. Send me Shadow."

He hoped that stressing the incompetence of the cartel men would diminish the blame he would receive. His masters were not forgiving, and his only hope to survive would be the deaths of the three Americans.

———

Jonathan, Cory, and Myron were scheduled to appear at police headquarters at 2:00 in the afternoon. Cory would be coming up from Lockheed in Sunnyvale. Jonathan had decided he and Cory had to reveal their connection with the Defense Intelligence Agency, but not to discuss details of their investigation. Myron would stick to his story that he was a friend of Jonathan and Cory and had agreed to pick them up at the airport.

When they arrived at the 1245 Third Street facility, they were separated and led to individual interrogation rooms. Shortly after Jonathan was seated, the two detectives who had been at the shooting scene entered the room, along with a woman who would be preparing the formal statement.

Detective Tosse nodded at Jonathan as he took a seat. "All right, please state your name for the record."

"Jonathan Scanlan."

"Why were you at the airport?"

"As I told you earlier, Cory Bishop and I were returning from a vacation on the Big Island."

"What was your involvement with the men trying to shoot you?"

"As I said earlier, I have no involvement with them."

"Come on Mr. Scanlan. The men were all members of the Sinaloa cartel. What is your connection to the cartel?"

"I have no involvement with any cartel. I'm a college professor and the author of several bestselling books."

This took the detective by surprise. "Are your books about the cartels?"

"Not at all."

The detective paused and glanced over at Detective Sartorio. "Can you think of anything that might have made you a target?"

Jonathan shrugged. "I don't see how there would be a connection, but Cory Bishop and I had been conducting an investigation with the Defense Intelligence Agency."

"What were you investigating?"

"It's classified, so I can't go into that, but our contact at the agency is a man named Forrest Woodward."

"Look Mr. Scanlan. This is serious. Three men are dead and a woman is in the hospital with a gunshot wound."

"If I told you the details of our investigation I would probably end up in Leavenworth. Call Woodward." Jonathan had to hide his smile, thinking about the unpleasant conversation Agent Woodward was about to have.

Jonathan was led to a waiting area after he signed his statement. Myron was already there. When Myron gave him a questioning look, Jonathan leaned close to the big man and said, "Let's talk about it when we get home."

Twenty minutes later, a woman led Cory to her friends. No one spoke until they were outside the building. Jonathan turned to Cory. "Do you want to come with us?"

"No, I'd rather just go home."

"Sure." Jonathan watched her as she walked away. For the first time, she seemed distant, and he wondered how the shooting was going to affect their relationship.

CHAPTER 33

Later that evening Cal joined Jonathan at his home, accompanied by Lamar Williams. While Cal and Jonathan huddled in Jonathan's office, Williams and Rossi waited in the kitchen.

Cal gave his friend a concerned look. "That was a close call. You know, it's all over the news."

Jonathan nodded. "I know. The local stations are all over it. I even saw a segment on Fox and CNN."

"Yeah. Attempted murder of a famous author. How's Cory handling it?"

"I'm afraid, not too well. When I called her, she basically cut me off."

Cal could see how the situation was affecting his friend. "Jesus, I feel awful. I'm the one who brought you and Cory into this mess."

"Don't blame yourself. We agreed to look for the leaker because it was the right thing to do. One thing I don't understand is, why are the cartels involved?"

Cal shook his head. "That's easy. The Chinese supply fentanyl to the cartels, which gives them leverage. It's a lot easier for cartel killers to get here from Mexico than to send guys from China."

Jonathan took a moment. "I'm sure you're right. I assume they're not going to stop."

Cal did not need to respond. Jonathan finally broke the uncomfortable silence. "How is your research coming on the support people at the Pentagon?"

"Nothing so far. I'm not finished, but the men and women I've looked at all seem normal. patriotic people."

Jonathan had a thought. "We may be further along than we think. Why else the over-the-top effort to take us out?"

Cal gave Jonathan's question some thought. "Well, they can't know what we know, or don't know. My guess is they believe we're still digging around and that's enough of a threat."

"Can I see the list of people?"

"Sure." Cal rummaged in his briefcase, finally producing several sheets of paper, which he handed to Jonathan.

Jonathan's eyes scanned the list of names. He stopped when he came across one name. "One of men on the list is Chinese, Joseph Wu."

"I know. I spent quite a bit of time checking him out. Chinese descent, but otherwise very American. Went to grammar school and high school in a suburb of Dallas, and then the University of Texas at Austin."

Jonathan sat back. "I guess looking for a Chinese guy leaking classified stuff to the Chinese would be a little too obvious."

Cal shrugged. "One would think. He's an aide to General Kelly."

Jonathan handed back the list. "I don't know what we can do next, other than trying to stay alive."

"You think they'll try again after the attempt on you here and the fiasco at the airport?"

"Unfortunately, I do. With the feds thinking they have their man, we're their only threat."

"That could change, if the Chinese react to another leak, it would clear Handy."

"It could, but after they got caught reacting to the fake brief, I believe they'll be more cautious."

"Have you heard from Woodward after the airport story broke?"

"No. I don't think he wants anything to do with us; he's going with Handy."

Cal looked across the coffee table at his friend. Something else was bothering Jonathan. "Jon, what is it?"

Jonathan turned away. "I don't know what you mean."

"Come on. You may be a decent poker player, but there's something else."

Jonathan finally looked down at the floor. "It's Cory."

"Because of the airport?"

Jonathan nodded. "It looks like she blames me for putting her at risk."

"She signed up for this."

"I know, but she didn't sign up to get shot at."

Cal was silent for a moment. "Are you guys breaking up?"

"I don't know, maybe. I'm worried that she thinks she can just walk away from us and she'll be safe. You and I know, that's not how it works. If they see an opening, they'll go after her. I know Myron has his man there, but if she ignores the threat…"

Cal studied his friend. I could talk to her, but I'm not sure it would help."

"No, it's something I have to do."

Cal felt Jonathan's pain as he and Lamar left for home.

CHAPTER 34

With a great deal of trepidation, Chan Wening picked up the secured phone. The voice of the minister was as clear as if he was sitting across from the head of Intelligence in his hotel room.

"Your attempt on Scanlan was botched,"

Wening could feel the sweat forming on his forehead. "Yes, the cartel people screwed it up. I need the best."

There was a very long pause. Jun finally said, "The man you requested is in Honduras, taking care of a politician that is opposing our efforts to control their rare earth resources. He will be in San Francisco in six days."

"Thank you."

"Chan, failure is not an option."

Chan Wening did not need a thesaurus to absorb the Ministers' meaning.

———

Jonathan was not an indecisive man, but at the moment, he was floundering as he mentally debated how to approach Cory. He had left several messages, none of which spurred a return call. Not sure what else to do, he decided to try a direct approach.

He found Myron watching television in the living room.

"Let's go for a ride."

"Sure, where to?"

"Cory's place in San Carlos."

"Okay, give me a minute." Myron went to his room, quickly returned, and looked out the front window at the street. "Our friends don't seem to be out there. Do you know if she'll be home?"

"No."

Myron gave him a look, but said nothing. They took Myron's Lincoln Continental, which had miraculously escaped damage at the airport. Neither man spoke during the ride. When they arrived, Myron stayed in the car as Jonathan walked to the building's entrance. He buzzed Cory's unit.

A moment later, her voice came over the speaker. "Who is this?"

"Jonathan."

There was no response for a long moment. Finally, Cory said, "Not now, Jonathan."

"Please, it's important. Just give me ten minutes."

Nothing happened for over a minute. Jonathan was about to walk away when the door unlocked. He took the stairs to her floor. Her door was open and when he walked in, he found Cory sitting on her sofa, her head bowed, as if she was studying her floor. Jim Stack was hovering near the kitchen.

Jonathan moved across the room until he was facing her. He stood awkwardly for a moment before taking a facing chair.

"I'm sorry. When Cal came to us, I didn't believe there was any danger in what we were doing. I was wrong." Cory remained silent, her face still averted. "If I could undo all this, I would, but I can't. If you never want to see me again, that's the way it'll be, but these people aren't going to go away."

She looked up. "What do you mean?"

"Until we expose the leaker, we all remain at risk. I believe their focus is mostly on Cal and me, but you also have to be careful." He paused for a moment, then said, "I love you."

Jonathan stood and left the condo.

CHAPTER 35

Circumstances had greatly changed Jonathan's normal routines. He no longer went for runs in the Presidio for obvious reasons. Hitting balls at the range or a round of golf was also felt to be too risky and hitting the city's restaurants was also ruled out. Myron walked Bo in the neighborhood.

A week had passed since his visit to Cory's condominium and there had been no word from the woman. Jonathan's state of mind was not in a good place with the realization that their relationship was over.

With no other outlet, Jonathan had set up a workout room in one of the bedrooms, which he and Myron used on a daily basis. He wanted to press Cal for his progress as his friend dug into the backgrounds of the Pentagon staff people, but he knew those kinds of calls would only divert his friend from his efforts.

He did think it odd that there did not appear to be people keeping his house under surveillance. He assumed they were out there, just being less obvious. When Cal had met with clients at their facilities, neither he or Lamar Williams had been aware of anyone following them.

Desperate for more information, Cal had gone online and obtained the name of the head of the Defense Intelligence Agency, a man named John E. Nichols. His efforts to reach the man had not been successful.

Jonathan's efforts to ask Gerald Lombardi at Homeland for additional help had gone unanswered.

It was midday, and Jonathan was puttering around the house when an idea came to him. He called Cal. When it went to voicemail, he asked his friend to call him back, using his cell. When Cal returned the call, Jonathan asked if he had an email address for the head of the DIA.

"What are you thinking?"

"Well, I know it's a Hail Mary, but I thought about sending him an email. Maybe it could get past the gatekeepers."

Cal thought for a moment. "Sure, why not."

Jonathan sat at his desk and began drafting a message he hoped could reach the man. He tore up several drafts before he thought he had one that might work.

Director Nichols

My name is Jonathan Scanlan. I worked with Agent Woodward in an attempt to locate the source of leaks at the Pentagon.

My associates, Cal Hulse, Cory Bishop, and I do not believe Colonel Handy is the source. We believe he was set up.

We have continued to investigate, and it appears our efforts have come to the attention of the Chinese. Before dismissing my claim, please check out the shooting at the San Francisco airport that occurred ten days ago. An attempt was made to kill Cory Bishop and myself.

Please contact me.

I hope to hear from you. Please use my cell phone, 415 555-4521, as my landline has been compromised.

Jonathan Scanlan

Four days later, Jonathan's cell chirped. The screen showed an unfamiliar number. Jonathan answered.

"Mr. Scanlan, this is Director Nichols at the Defense Intelligence Agency."

"Good afternoon, Director."

"I received your email and did some checking, anyway enough to take you seriously. Why do you believe Colonel Handy hasn't been leaking information?"

"I interviewed Handy. He would be too smart to have incriminating information on his home computer, and then there is the time stamp on the entry."

"What about the time stamp?"

"The information was entered after we did our interviews and nine days after the fake brief was released. That doesn't make sense."

"I looked into the shooting at the airport. The shooters were cartel men."

"Yes, and the Chinese have a connection to the Sinaloa cartel."

There was a long pause and, for a moment, Jonathan thought he had lost the connection. "Your email mentioned that your landline has been compromised."

"Yes, it still is. We also found that my home was bugged. We have the devices if you wish to see them."

"No, that's not necessary. How soon can you be in DC?"

Jonathan thought for a moment. "I'm working with Cal Hulse on this. Would you like him to come?"

"Perhaps later."

"I could leave tomorrow."

"A ticket will be waiting for you at United for the midday flight."

It took a moment for Jonathan to realize the director had ended the call. Jonathan immediately called Cal and left a message that he was on his way to DC.

CHAPTER 36

With the five-hour flight and time change, Jonathan did not reach his hotel until early evening. A text message on his phone informed him that his meeting with the head of the agency was set at 10;00 the following morning.

He had an early dinner at the restaurant at the hotel, called for an eight o'clock wake-up call, and watched television in his room until he finally fell asleep. While he was optimistic about the meeting with the director, he had no idea what the man planned to tell him.

In the morning, when he went down to the lobby, he asked how long it would take to reach the DIA facility in DC. The concierge told him, with traffic, to plan on thirty minutes. He had time for coffee and a muffin before heading out the door. He took a cab and arrived at the Joint Base Anacostia-Bolling headquarters complex ten minutes early.

The size of the facility shocked him. He expected a large building, but the building was enormous. He assumed it had to house thousands of people.

He expected security would be tight and he was not disappointed. His identification was verified before a visitor's pass was issued. After passing through a magnetometer. he was asked to get into a cart with a driver-escort. The ride into the building included rising several floors in a large elevator.

When they arrived at the top floor, the escort led him to a waiting area. He approached a woman at a reception desk, identified himself and took a seat. Within minutes a relatively short man of about fifty approached him and offered his hand.

"John Nichols."

Jonathan stood and shook the man's hand. He had assumed the head of the agency would be an older version of Forrest Woodward. Nichols looked more like a well-dressed accountant.

Nichols led him to his private office, which was quite spacious with modern furnishings, but, Jonathan noticed, no personal touches.

He motioned Jonathan toward the visitor's chairs and took a seat behind a large, glass topped desk. "I imagine you're wondering why I asked you to come here."

Jonathan thought it had been more like a summons, but smiled and said, "Yes. I'm also wondering why I'm not meeting with a midlevel staffer."

The director's smile vanished, replaced with a serious frown. "It's because we're not dealing with a midlevel problem. I reviewed the file on Handy, and I have to agree with you. I don't think he's the leaker, which means we haven't solved the problem."

When Jonathan did not respond, Nichols leaned forward. "As I mentioned, you've been thoroughly checked out. I don't believe you and your friends have stopped investigating. What have you found out?"

Jonathan studied the man for a moment. "We believe one of the Pentagon staff people is a mole."

"Have you identified the mole?"

"No. We've looked at about twenty people and, so far, nothing pops out."

"Why do you think an attempt was made on your life?"

"Actually, there were two attempts. The first was when I went out for a run near my home. Two men, I believe Hispanic, tried to shoot me."

"Did you report it?"

"No, I didn't see the point. When they missed and took off, I couldn't have identified them or even their car. After that we hired protection, which turned out to have been a worthwhile investment."

"That would be Myron Rossi."

"Yes, and two other men to cover Cal Hulse and Cory Bishop."

Nichols offered a faint smile. "I've read your three books."

"I hope you enjoyed them."

"Interesting reading. I don't imagine you're terribly popular with the FBI."

"Maybe not in DC, but I'm fine with the San Francisco office."

"I understand you weren't willing to sign a confidentiality agreement."

"No, I wasn't. I'm a writer. If there's a story, I want to write about it."

The director thought for a moment. "Should there be a story, would you agree for us to edit it for sensitive information?"

"I would agree for it to be edited for anything that would hurt the country, but not for anything that might bruise egos or point out incompetence."

Nichols thought for a moment. "We can live with that." He picked up his phone and began giving instructions. It was apparent to Jonathan that the person on the other end of the line was arguing against the director's instructions. He heard Nichols say, "Just do it," before he hung up.

The director looked at Jonathan. "You'll need to sign some documents before I can give you more information. How about some coffee while we wait for them to arrive?"

"Sure. How long have you been the director at DIA?"

"About three and a half years."

After a short wait a young woman entered the office, carrying a tray containing two mugs, a carafe, cream and sweeteners. Nichols thanked the woman and came around his desk to pour the coffee. He pointed to the cream and sweeteners, which Jonathan declined.

"Grab your mug, let's go sit over here."

After twenty minutes of polite conversation, a man knocked at the door and came in with several forms. He seemed somewhat put out as he handed the paperwork to Nichols. When the man had left, the director handed the forms to Jonathan and said, "My aide didn't care for the modifications I added to the confidentiality agreement. Read it over and sign it if it meets your terms."

After a few minutes, Jonathan looked up. "It's fine." He took out a pen and began signing the forms. He handed the paperwork back to Nicols and said, "I'd like a copy of these."

"No problem. From your investigation you know what we're up against. There is one thing you're not aware of. We believe there is a second leaker. In addition to someone at the Pentagon, we are quite sure there is a second source, either at State or the White House."

Jonathan sat back and stared at the director. "How did you reach this conclusion?"

Nichols rubbed his forehead and glanced out his window toward the Potomac, which Jonathan read as a stress related tell. "The Pentagon leaks are all related to briefing information going to the Joint Chiefs. The other leak relates to our posture in the Middle East."

"Iran?"

"Could be. It also could be Russia or someone else that doesn't like our involvement in the region."

"You understand, I'll be working with Cal Hulse on this."

"What about Cory Bishop?"

"I'm not sure about Cory. She was very shaken by the shooting at the airport."

Nichols nodded. "I understand. Your credentials will give you unlimited access. Before you leave, I'll introduce you to your main contact. You can also reach me if you find roadblocks."

"Forrest Woodward?"

The director smiled. "No, Mr. Woodward won't be involved." Director Nichols stood and went around his desk. He picked up his phone and made a short call. Jonathan stood, believing the meeting was over. Moments later a dark-haired woman knocked and came in the room.

"Jonathan Scanlan this is Carolyn Staten. Agent Staten will be your primary contact."

Jonathan stepped forward and offered his hand, which Ms. Staten shook.

Nichols smiled and turned to Jonathan and his new workmate. "Carolyn, why don't you two get acquainted, and please provide Mr.

Scanlan with whatever he needs." Obviously, a signal that the meeting was over.

Agent Staten led Jonathan out of the office and down the hall to a small conference room.

When they were seated, Jonathan said, "I assume you've been briefed about the problem."

"Yes, and please call me Carolyn."

"The Agency pulled their computer and communications gear out when we were told the investigation was over. Can you arrange for that equipment to be replaced?"

"Of course. Mr. Hulse will be receiving everything tomorrow."

"Let's go with first names, Jonathan and Cal."

Jonathan realized Carolyn had a beautiful smile. The smile quickly disappeared as her expression turned serious. "Do you and Cal have a plan? And is Cory Bishop still involved?"

"The shootout at the San Francisco airport has badly shaken Cory. I don't know if she wishes to continue to be involved. I can't say we really have a plan. We're looking at about twenty aides and staffers at the Pentagon. I just heard about the second leak."

Jonathan could tell Carolyn was hoping for a more robust game plan. "Where are you staying?"

"At the St. Regis."

Carolyn sat back, as if he had just struck her. "The St. Regis, we can't afford that."

"You're not paying for my room. Besides, I'll be flying back home tomorrow."

"Tomorrow? I thought we'd be working the investigation immediately."

"We are. But first we have to figure out what we're going to do. I'll be doing that with Cal. You can join us in San Francisco if you like. If you want, you can stay at my house, it's quite large."

This was obviously not what Carolyn Staten expected. "I don't know. I guess I can join you out there in a couple of days."

Carolyn gave Jonathan her contact information and, with little confidence in her new workmate, escorted Jonathan from the building.

CHAPTER 37

Chan Wening was in his hotel room when there was a knock on his door. When he opened the door, an Asian man of middle size and middle years, dressed in casual clothes, stared at him in silence. The man's face was unfamiliar to the head of Intelligence.

"Yes?"

"You sent for me." The man spoke with a Beijing dialect.

Wening realized the man in the doorway was known as Shadow. He waved the man into the room. "Have you been briefed?"

"Only that Beijing wants three people eliminated."

Wening picked up his briefcase and extracted a file. "Background information on the three individuals."

The man took the file, but made no effort to review its contents. Wening said, "Let me have the number where I can reach you."

"I will call you if I need additional information." The man left the room, closing the door quietly behind him.

Wening stood, staring at the door. He felt a chill, as if a cold wind had swept through the room. As the head of Intelligence, he demanded respect, and even fear from those below him. It was Chan Wening who felt the cold hand of fear.

———

Jonathan arrived home after a midday flight. He had briefed Cal the prior evening and arranged a meeting the following day. While Cal took their renewed involvement with DIA as a major success, Jonathan was more circumspect. Finding the leaker among twenty aides and staffers was definitely a needle-in-a-haystack situation, and he had no plan for locating the other mole.

He had made it clear, through Carolyn, that their focus was on the Pentagon leaker. They did not have the time and resources to also look for the one involving the Middle East.

During his flight, he had given thought to working with Carolyn. She appeared to be highly intelligent and highly motivated. While he was not attracted to her, he found her to be attractive, but a woman who downplayed her physical appearance, probably intentionally.

While Myron assured him that no one appeared to be keeping the house under surveillance, Jonathan was hesitant to go for a run. Eventually, cabin fever won. He loaded Bo into his Jeep and drove away from the house, keeping an eye on his rear-view mirror. When he was sure he was not being followed, he doubled back and parked several blocks from his home, allowing him to enter the Presidio at a new location.

After the first mile, Jonathan could feel the effect of his lack of conditioning. Bo was happy, even though Jonathan did not cover his usual five miles.

Cal arrived just after three in the afternoon. They met in the room Jonathan had set up as an office. Myron and Lamar Williams grabbed a couple of beers and went out into the backyard. Cal handed Jonathan the file on the Pentagon staffers and aides. Jonathan scanned the material, seeing nothing of interest.

When he surfaced, Cal shrugged. "I know, nothing stands out."

Jonathan thought for a moment. "You know, Cory came up with the idea that a traitor wouldn't be contributing to military-oriented charities. It didn't really pan out, but it did help us narrow the search. Is there something we can focus on like that?"

Cal shook his head. "I don't know. The people on our list don't make much money, so I'm not sure they would be making contributions."

"They wouldn't be making significant contributions, but maybe small ones, like fifty dollars."

Cal gave it some thought. "Maybe, it's worth looking into."

Jonathan glanced at his friend. "Have you seen anyone keeping tabs on you?"

"No, and Lamar hasn't seen anyone."

"I don't understand. They have to assume we're still a threat. After trying to shoot me here and then at the airport, why would they back off?"

"I agree. It doesn't make sense."

"Corolyn Staten should be arriving later today. I think you'll like working with her."

Cal shrugged and looked down at his files. "So, Cory's out of it?"

"I guess so. I haven't heard from her."

Cal looked up at his friend. "Are you okay with that?"

"No, but I don't know what I can do about it. I told her how I felt."

When Lamar drove Cal home, neither man noticed the gray sedan that followed two blocks behind.

Hai Li knew where Cal Hulse was going. He had already studied the condominium complex on Pacific Avenue. While the building had above average security, he knew he could easily breach the systems. He also did not view the man protecting Hulse as a serious problem. He had assassinated many with far greater security.

He planned to kill Hulse and Scanlan when they were together. Taking out one, would alert the other to the threat and make his task much more difficult. From what he had been told, the Bishop woman was not the same level of threat.

He smiled at being called Shadow. While quite ridiculous, it cloaked him as an almost mythical angel of death and greatly enhanced the compensation he received for his services. It also tended to protect him from micromanagement by the fools who employed him.

When Hulse and his protector entered the Pacific Heights building, he saw no value in continuing surveillance and headed back to his hotel.

CHAPTER 38

Jonathan's cell chirped as he was scanning the Chronicle and sipping the last of his coffee. He had earlier programmed Carolyn Staten into his contact list and saw her name on the screen.

"Morning, Carolyn. How was your flight?"

"The flight was fine. When can we get together?"

"Well, I assume you mean Cal and me. Cal's not a morning person. I'll give him a call and let you know. Where are you staying?"

"The Holiday Inn on Van Ness."

"Okay, I'll call you as soon as I can reach him."

Jonathan called Cal and left a message. An hour later his friend returned the call. "All right, why don't we meet at my place at eleven."

Jonathan and Myron arrived fifteen minutes early, had some coffee and waited for Agent Staten. She buzzed Cal's unit at exactly eleven.

Cal looked at Jonathan as he buzzed her into the building. "Prompt lady."

When Carolyn Staten walked into Cal condominium, she seemed puzzled by the array of sports-related collectibles in the unit. She also noticed Lamaar Williams and Myron Rossi in the kitchen.

When Jonathan introduced Cal, Carolyn formally stepped forward and shook his hand. "I'm pleased to meet you. Can I ask, who are these men?" As she waved in the direction of Myron and Lamar.

Jonathan said, "We've employed Myron and Lamar to protect us. Another man is with Cory Bishop."

Carolyn was visibly upset. "We're dealing with highly classified information. They don't have clearance to be involved in our investigation."

Jonathan shook his head. "They're not involved in the investigation. Their job is to keep us alive. Myron shot two of the men who were trying to kill Cory and me at the airport. Guys, why don't you go watch television while we have our meeting?"

Myron and Lamar left the room, which seemed to partially appease the DIA agent. Cal said, "Let's go over here and let you review what we've been able to dig up on the Pentagon personnel."

Cal pushed a large file folder across the table. Carolyn began reading the contents while Jonathan refilled his coffee mug. When he asked if she would like a cup, she declined.

After an hour, Carolyn looked up. "Interesting information, but I don't see anything that will help us."

"I agree. Jonathan and I have been trying to come up with something that can help us narrow down the list." Cal then described Cory's idea of eliminating individuals who had contributed to military-related charities.

Carolyn looked up at Cal. "How would you have access to that type of information?"

Cal said, in an even tone, "I don't think you need to know that."

Carolyn shot up, almost overturning her chair. "I won't be party to illegal activities."

As she started to leave, Jonathan said, "Before you leave, I suggest you call Director Nicholes and explain your problem."

This stopped Agent Staten in midstride. She fumbled her phone out of her purse and moved away from Jonathan and Cal as she placed the call, which took several minutes. When the call ended, she moved to one of the living room chairs and sat down. Her face displayed her discomfort.

Jonathan said, "Okay, now that we've gotten past that issue, help us figure out what we can do to narrow the search."

Cal stepped in. "Let's see what comes up when I look at the charitable deductions. Any other ideas?"

Jonathan glanced at a somewhat deflated DIA agent. "Let's think about it and get together tomorrow. Carolyn, did you rent a car?"

She gave Jonathan a puzzled look. "No, I took a cab."

"All right, come on, Myron and I'll give you a ride back to your hotel."

———

Hai Li sat in his car a half block from Cal's building. He had been tempted to slip into the building and kill everyone in Cal's unit. He was confident he could have pulled it off, but killing five people, at least two of whom would be armed, would have been a challenge.

He had taken a photo of the woman, who he knew was not Cory Bishop. Later, he would transmit it to Beijing and ask for her to be identified.

He knew there would be better opportunities to complete his mission.

CHAPTER 39

L ater, after Carolyn had been dropped off, Jonathan called Cal. He was surprised when his friend picked up. "What do you think of Agent Staten?"

"She's bright, but I'm not sure she's done this type of work before."

"You may be right. At least we now have a conduit into the DIA. What's your schedule like tomorrow?"

"I'll be working late tonight, looking at deductions on everyone's tax filings, so not too early."

"How about 10:30 at my place?"

"That'll work."

When he called Carolyn and told her about the meeting, she sounded frustrated. "10:30, that's ridiculous. I came here to work, not waste my morning sitting around my hotel."

"I understand, but Cal will have been working all night on the charitable donation angle."

There was a pause before a more conciliatory Carolyn said, "Sorry. I'll see you at 10:30."

When Carolyn arrived a few minutes early, she stood in the entry admiring Jonathan's home. "This is beautiful, the writing business must be really rewarding."

"It is, but not all of this came from my books."

"Inheritance?"

"No, would you like coffee?"

Realizing she had overstepped, she nodded. Jonathan led her into his kitchen and poured her a cup. He pointed to a plate of muffins, but she declined.

Cal came in with Lamar. Jonathan suggested the man could have coffee and a muffin and join Myron outside. Jonathan and his guests moved to his study, huddling together around a coffee table.

Cal set a file folder on the table. "Quite a few of the people we're looking at made donations to military type charities. The donated amounts were small, as these are not highly paid folks. Only eight did not do that type of donation."

Jonathan smiled at his friend. "That really helps."

Carolyn glanced at the two men. "So, you think a traitor wouldn't support one of these charities?"

Jonathan said, "Why would someone who is selling out his or her country donate to something like Tunnels to Towers?"

She thought for a moment before nodding agreement. "I had a thought last night. Think about the leaker. Wouldn't the person avoid having close friends or socialize with his or her coworkers?"

Cal and Jonathan gave her comment some thought. She added, "Wouldn't the risk be too great. Close friends share personal information."

Cal nodded. "You're probably right. Being a loner doesn't mean you're a traitor, but close friends would bullshit about personal stuff, like what they did in high school or summer vacations."

Jonathan leaned back in his chair. "Great thinking, Carolyn. Coupled with the donation information we can really narrow the list."

Carolyn blushed slightly and smiled. "Thank you."

When Jonathan went into the kitchen for a coffee refill, Carolyn turned to Cal. "I'm sorry about yesterday."

Cal, who tended to be somewhat awkward around women, stammered, "Don't be. I understand how my methods would bother you."

When Jonathan returned, he could sense a change in the relationship, but said nothing. He sat down and asked Carolyn, "Can you have someone at DIA nose around the people on our list to see if there is anyone without close friends?"

"Absolutely."

CHAPTER 40

The information came back surprisingly quickly. Five people on the list of twenty either did not appear to have close friends or were, to some degree, antisocial. Two were individuals who had donated to veteran or other military-related charities. The other three were Carlos Bourdet, Joyce Galvin, and Joseph Wu. All three were civilian employees.

Bourdet was a thirty-two-year-old unmarried man from Encino, California. He was a graduate from UCLA with a Bachelor of Science and a master's degree in finance. He is on Colonel Thomas Dogerty's staff. Joyce Galvin hailed from upstate New York, possessed a bachelor's degree from Brown, and is an aide to General William Hamlin. Galvin is unmarried, twenty-eight years old, and has worked at the Pentagon for six years.

Joseph Wu was twenty-seven and also unmarried. Wu was born and raised in a suburb of Dallas and had a bachelor's degree from the University of Texas. He had worked at the State Department for slightly less than three years before moving to the Pentagon. He is an aide to General Michael Kelly.

Carolyn, Cal, and Jonathan studied the information on the woman and the two men for some time.

Jonathan looked across the table at Carolyn and Cal. "What do you think?"

Cal stared off into space for a moment. "I don't know. Our criteria, in retrospect, might be a little weak. We're down to these three people because they didn't make donations and aren't very social."

Carolyn seemed a little lost. "I don't know. When you put it that way it does sound weak. We certainly couldn't bring charges on this."

Jonathan shook his head. "You're right, but it's all we have. These three people could be totally clean, but unless we come up with another approach, let's give them a closer look."

Cal looked at his friend. "What do you propose?"

"We didn't get anywhere when Cory and I interviewed the nine officers. So, let's not go with a direct approach. But what if Carolyn and I talk to people who knew these three in high school and college, and talk to their families?"

Cal shrugged. "Worth a try."

Carolyn also seemed less than optimistic. "Okay, when do you want to do this?"

"I'll start making calls. Let's plan on taking off on Wednesday."

———

News that the Defense Intelligence Agency was asking questions about a select group of aides and staffers at the Pentagon was quickly known in Beijing. This information was immediately transmitted to Chan Wening, who was still in San Francisco.

The directive was clear: Scanlan and Hulse must be eliminated immediately. This left Chan Wening in an awkward position. The man they called Shadow had refused to provide his cell number. Admitting this to Beijing would be viewed as a sign of weakness, and, as the head of Intelligence, that weakness might prove fatal.

In the tradition of virtually all bureaucrats, Wening decided to lie. He responded to Beijing, saying the number Shadow had given him was wrong, and he needed the correct contact number.

He was relieved when, moments later, a text arrived with the contact number.

Wening dialed the number. When it was answered, the man simply said, "Yes?"

"The Minister of National Defense requires the immediate elimination of Jonathan Scanlan and Cal Hulse." There was no reply. Shadow had hung up.

Hai Li was sitting on a bench in the Presidio with a view of Jonathan's home. He returned his phone to his pocket and sighed. This is how operations fail. Bureaucrats panicked and demanded immediate action, without adequate planning. Unfortunately, when the master calls, the dog comes.

He did not believe he had time to wait for an opportunity to take out Scanlan and Hulse when they were together. As he stood up and walked back to where he had parked his car, he concluded that he would initially focus on Scanlan.

The following day, he received a text message telling him that Scanlan had booked two round-trip tickets to the Los Angeles International Airport, leaving on Wednesday, with an open return.

Hai Li immediately booked a ticket on the same airline, only for a flight arriving two hours before Scanlan's. Knowing he could not bring a weapon on board, he called Wening and gave him instructions on the weapon he wanted on his arrival.

CHAPTER 41

Carolyn met Jonathan at his home to discuss their upcoming trip. When he heard the agenda, Myron insisted on joining them in Los Angeles.

Jonathan was not at all sure Myron's presence was necessary, but then he thought about SFO. "All right, I'll book your ticket."

"No, I'm licensed to carry, but I want to have more than my Glock, and it's a pain to get it through TSA. I'll leave on Tuesday, drive down, and meet you at the airport."

Carolyn watched this exchange and asked, "You think this is necessary?"

Jonathan shrugged. "Probably not, but better safe than sorry. Excuse me, I need to make arrangements for Bo."

Jonathan had been given the number of a woman who had a dog-sitting service. After a brief conversation with the woman, named Denise Osmao, Bo's plans were set.

Carolyn asked Jonathan who they would be meeting with when they got to Los Angeles.

"We have appointments to meet with Carlos Bourdet's parents and his UCLA counselor."

Carolyn nodded and made a few notes.

Jonathan offered to pick Carolyn up at her hotel on the way to the airport, but she declined. She did agree to meet him at the United ticket counter.

On Wednesday morning, Jonathan took an Uber to the airport. It was a clear, cloudless day and traffic was light, allowing him to arrive with plenty of time for his flight. Carolyn had arrived even earlier and was waiting in the lobby by the United ticket counters.

The flight left on time for the short hop to LAX. As Jonathan and Carolyn took their seats, Jonathan had a flashback to Cory's white-knuckle flight to the East Coast. An hour later, they were gathering their carry-on bags and making their way off the plane.

As they followed the flow of people moving toward the terminal's exit, neither Jonathan nor Carolyn noticed the middle-aged, average-looking, Asian man who followed them. When they had cleared the secured area and were passing through baggage claim, another Asian man approached Hai Li. Without a word, he handed Shadow a daypack.

Hai Li unzipped the daypack and casually slipped his hand inside. He suppressed a grim smile as he felt the familiar shape of a Sig Sauer P938 with an attached suppressor. Once outside the terminal, he planned to kill Scanlan and the woman. He had arranged for a car and driver to be waiting to drive him away. The car had been stolen earlier in the day and would be destroyed after his escape.

He had clicked off the safety and was about to pull the gun from the pack when a huge man stepped away from a large car, momentarily blocking his view of Scanlan and the woman. The big man opened the Lincoln Continental's rear door for the woman as Scanlan slipped into the front passenger seat.

He could have taken a shot at his targets but remembered that a large man had shot two of the cartel killers at the San Francisco airport. Not all plans worked to perfection. He clicked on the pistol's safety and walked to the car he had intended to use for his escape.

He turned to the driver and pointed at the black Lincoln. "Follow that car."

Myron pulled away from the curb and into the heavily congested traffic, leaving the airport. A moment later, the silver Honda and the two men followed.

The predictable bumper-to-bumper Los Angeles traffic made following the Lincoln child's play. After twenty miles and forty minutes, the Lincoln turned into a Marriott Courtyard on Ventura in Sherman Oaks.

The Honda pulled into the parking lot and waited as Myron popped the trunk and handed Jonathan and Carolyn their roller bags. He then pulled away from the entrance and turned into the parking area. Hai Li and his driver ducked down as the Lincoln passed.

Hai Li did not want to be seen while Scanlan and the woman were checking in. After several minutes, he turned to the driver. "Lose the car." He pulled his overnight bag from the rear seat and walked to the hotel entrance. A quick glance inside showed Scanlan and the woman had left the lobby. He went to the reception desk and asked politely if rooms were available, and apologized for not having made a reservation. He explained that his trip had been a last-minute thing.

The clerk smiled and said there was no problem. Hai Li provided a California driver's license under the name Winston Chow and a matching credit card. Within minutes, he was on his way to his room.

When Myron had turned into the Marriott property, Carolyn had said, "I can't stay here. This is way more expensive than my expense guidelines allow."

Jonathan shook his head. "We need to all be at the same hotel and we're not staying at Motel Six. Besides, I'm paying for this."

Carolyn stared at him for a moment. "I don't understand."

"Look, there's nothing to really understand. I can afford to pay for this and whatever other expenses come up. Call John Nichols if this is a problem>"

"Is Myron also staying here?"

"Yes, I reserved three rooms."

———

Hai Li sat in his room and considered how best to kill Scanlan. He considered simply knocking on the man's door and shooting him when he answered. Not elegant, but sometimes the simplest path was the best. Of course, he would first have to find out which room was Scanlan's.

CHAPTER 42

Hai Li knew Scanlan, and probably the woman, would be using this trip to meet various people. He called Hertz and asked if a rental could be delivered to his hotel. He was assured that there was no problem and, after he provided his name of the day and credit card, he was told his rental would be delivered within the hour.

The following morning, he was sitting in a light blue Toyota Camry parked two rows away from Myron's Lincoln Continental. Hai Li watched Myron, Carolyn, and Jonathan leave the hotel and walk to the Lincoln. He waited until they had driven out of the parking lot and onto Ventura Boulevard. There was no need to keep them in sight. He had placed a tracking device inside the Lincoln's rear bumper.

Fifteen minutes later, Li found the Lincoln parked in front of a well-maintained, two-story home on Haskell Avenue in Encino Village. The big man was sitting in the driver's seat. Hai Li drove past until he was two blocks away, turned his rental around, and parked almost a block away with a view of the home.

———

Carolyn and Jonathan walked up to the home and rang the doorbell. A slender middle-aged woman answered the door, offering a tentative smile. "Mr. Scanlan and Ms. Staten?"

Jonathan offered his hand. "Jonathan and Carolyn, please."

"Please come in." She led them into a comfortable living room.

A short man put down his newspaper and rose from his chair. "Joseph Bourdet, and you met my wife, Teresa. When you called, you said you're with the Defense Intelligence Agency. Can I ask what this is about?"

Jonathan took the lead. "Nothing important. Your son, Carlos, has a high-level security position and we simply want to be sure all the information in his file is accurate."

While Teresa Bourdet seemed comfortable with this explanation, her husband appeared somewhat wary. "Can I see your identification?"

"Certainly." Both Jonathan and Carolyn offered their agency-provided credentials. This seemed to satisfy the man.

Carolyn glanced at her notes. "Just to confirm our information. Carlos attended Ferrahian High School. Then went on to UCLA, where he graduated with a Bachelor of Science and an MBA."

Both parents simply nodded. Jonathan asked, "Did Carlos participate in any other activities while he was at UCLA, such as sports or clubs, like the debate society?"

Joseph shook his head. "No, not really. Carlos was not interested in sports. I don't believe he joined any clubs." He added proudly, "He graduated with straight As."

Jonathan and Carolyn stretched out their visit with a number of inane questions before closing their files, thanking the Bourdets, and leaving the house.

As they walked back to the car, Carolyn asked, "Anything?"

Jonathan just shook his head.

With time to kill before their next meeting, Jonathan suggested they find a coffee shop. Carolyn pulled out her cell and provided Myron with directions to a Starbucks a mile away.

After their coffee and muffins, Myron drove them to the sprawling UCLA campus tucked
into the base of the Santa Monica Mountains.

After parking in the visitor's lot, Jonathan and Carolyn made their way to the visitor's center. They were given directions to the Anderson School of Management. Jonathan had made an appointment with a man named Dmitry Spohn, who had been Carlos Bourdet's counselor.

Professor Spohn turned out to be an affable man of about forty. The business school counselor was of medium height with the physique of a man who worked out regularly. Jonathan thanked the man for taking the time to meet with them and introduced Carolyn.

"Glad to help. You said this was about Carlos."

"Yes. As you probably know, Carlos is employed at the Department of Defense and has an extremely high security rating. We periodically do background checks on all the personnel who handle sensitive information. We know he did very well academically. Can you tell us anything about his outside interests or activities?"

Spohn thought for a moment. "Not really. I'm not aware that he had any outside activities. As you said, he was an excellent student. Carlos tended to be somewhat shy. That probably limited his interest in participating in outside activities."

Jonathan and Carolyn chatted with Spohn for several more minutes, gaining no additional insight into Carlos, thanked the man, and returned to their car.

Hai Li sat in his rental forty yards away from the Lincoln. The UCLA campus was obviously not the place to shoot Jonathan Scanlan and the woman. He was confident there would be better opportunities.

CHAPTER 43

When they returned to their hotel, they all went to their separate rooms to make calls. They agreed to meet in the lobby at seven and go to dinner together. Jonathan called Cal and filled him in on their unproductive outing.

Jonathan had made reservations at La Dolce Vita in Beverly Hills. Believing parking would be a problem, they took an Uber to the restaurant. When they were seated, Jonathan ordered a glass of Chardonnay, Myron a beer, and Carolyn a club soda with a lime. Jonathan wondered if the DIA woman was a nondrinker or if she thought she should not drink alcohol when she was on the job.

Hai Li followed the Uber car into Beverly Hills. He found parking to be nearly impossible as he cruised Santa Monica Boulevard. He finally found a yellow loading space and quickly pulled into it. As he was using a false name for the rental, he couldn't care less if the car was ticketed. It was Friday night, and the area was extremely crowded. The crowds were a mixed blessing. While they provided great cover, there was a good chance he would be photographed by someone's cell phone.

He had not anticipated the need for a disguise, and certainly did not want to be the subject of a manhunt. He pulled a daypack from the back seat and pawed through it. He pulled out a baseball cap and a pair of sunglasses. Not enough to change his features. Then he found a blue

COVID-type face mask. He placed his silenced Sig Sauer in the bag. His parking space was too far from the restaurant to see the entrance, which created an additional problem

If he waited outside the restaurant, he could easily kill the two men and the woman when they left. He would then have to hustle almost a full city block, through a crowded sidewalk, back to his car. Not feasible.

Frustrated, he shoved the cap, sunglasses, and mask back into the pack and returned the gun to his pocket. He drove back to the hotel, planning to find out Scanlan's room number and kill him there.

After an excellent dinner, Jonathan had called for an Uber ride for a return to the Marriott. Carolyn had made an effort to pay for her dinner, which Jonathan brushed aside.

They agreed to return to San Francisco the following day. Jonathan would set up meetings similar to those in Encino for Joyce Galvin and Joseph Wu's families and contacts.

Hai Li knew, from the information he had been provided, that Jonathan Scanlan drank alcohol in moderation. He had no idea what type of alcohol the man preferred. On the way back to the hotel, he had stopped at a liquor store and purchased a bottle of Domaine Carneros Brut Cuvee and a gift bag.

He lingered in the café at the hotel with a view of the lobby. When he saw Jonathan, the woman, and the big man return and make their way to the elevators, he paid his check and went to his room. He packed his few personal items and took them down to his car. Returning to his room, he wiped the room down, removing his fingerprints from anything he had touched.

He then went down to the lobby and asked the concierge to deliver the bottle of bubbly to Jonathan Scanlan's room.

Moments later, a hotel employee was given the bottle and set off to deliver it to Scanlan's room. Hai Li followed the man at a discreet distance. He had no choice but to join the young man when he entered one of the elevators. The man pushed the button for the third floor and looked inquiringly at Hai Li, who smiled and said, "Same floor."

When they stepped out of the elevator, the young man went to the right and Hai Li to the left. After a brief pause, Hai Li turned around and followed the employee down the hall at a distance. As soon as the young man knocked on room 318's door, Hai Li quickly walked back and took the stairs to his room on the second floor.

When Jonathan answered the knock on his door, the young man handed him the bottle. Jonathan was confused. "I don't understand. Who is this from?"

"I have no idea, sir."

Jonathan could see that there was no note. He tipped the employee and set the bottle on a table. He went to the connecting door and knocked. When Myron opened the door, Jonathan pointed to the bottle.

"This was just delivered. There's no note, and who knows we're here? Other than you, Carolyn, and Cal, nobody knows where we're staying."

Myron thought for a moment. "Are you and Carolyn, you know, sort of an item?"

Jonathan laughed. "Hardly."

"Just in case, call her room."

Jonathan walked over, picked up the hotel phone and asked to be connected to Carolyn Staten's room."

She picked up on the first ring. "Carolyn, Jonathan. I know this is an odd question, but did you send a bottle of Champagne to my room?"

Carolyn was indignant. "Of course not."

"Look, the only reason I asked is that Cal, you, and Myron are the only people who know we're staying here, so I had to ask."

In a more measured tone, Carolyn said, "You'll have to ask Myron and Cal," before she hung up.

Jonathan turned to Myron. "This is weird, I don't even care for Champaign."

Myron's street smarts kicked in. "Call down to the desk. Tell them you need to change your room immediately."

Myron began throwing Jonathan's clothes and toiletries into his roller suitcase. Jonathan was staring at his friend as if the man had gone insane. "What are you doing?"

"Saving your ass. Make the call. Tell them to bring the new room keys to my room."

Myron took a quick look around the room, checking to see if he had missed anything, closed the suitcase, and pulled Jonathan and his roller into his connecting room.

Once inside, Myron closed and locked the connecting door. Jonathan was still staring at the big man.

"What?"

"Think about it. If someone, i.e., a bad guy, wanted to know your room number, how would they get it? The hotel wouldn't give out that information. How about they have the hotel send a bottle of wine to your room, follow the delivery guy and, guess what, they have your room number."

Jonathan shook his head. "I don't know. I think you're overreacting."

"If I am, no big deal. If I'm right, it's a big deal."

Ten minutes later, a uniformed hotel employee knocked on Myron's door. The young man handed Myron new room keys in a paper sleeve. Jonathan's new room was on the same floor, several doors down.

"What now?"

"We wait." Jonathan sat on the chair in front of the room's small desk, and Myron sat on the edge of the bed.

"Why don't I go to my new room?"

"If I'm right, things are going to happen very soon, and you wouldn't want to be out in the hallway when it comes down."

Twenty minutes later, they heard someone knocking on the door to Jonathan's, now vacant, room.

Myron stepped to the door to his room, holding his Glock. He opened it slowly and peeked around the door frame. An Asian man was standing in front of Jonathan's room.

Myron kept his body inside his room when he leaned his head out and asked, "Can we help you?"

Hai Li turned toward Myron and smiled. In a swift motion, he brought his gun up and began firing. Myron dropped to the floor, reached his hand outside his door, and, without aiming, fired off two shots.

Hai Li fired several more shots as he backed quickly down the hall before darting into the stairway.

While Hai Li had used a silencer, Myron had not, and the gunshots were deafening. Several guests in nearby rooms were shouting, although none opened their doors.

Jonathan, who had thrown himself on the floor, stood up. "Do you think you hit him?"

"No chance. I only fired to let him know we were armed."

"So, what now?"

"We wait for the police. You might want to call Carolyn and ask her to join us."

Carolyn arrived moments before the police. The first officers came in with guns drawn. They quickly realized Myron, Jonathan, and Carolyn were victims. Nevertheless, they took Myron's pistol and called in for help.

Two detectives and several more uniforms arrived. Jonathan and Carolyn produced their credentials, and Myron showed them his private investigator's license and permit to carry. The lead detective introduced himself as Detective Richard Ahrens and his partner as Detective Philip Pedder.

Ahrens glanced at the shot-up doorway. "Somebody really doesn't like you. Did you see the shooter?"

Myron said. "Only a glance before I was on the floor, trying not to get shot. Middle-aged Asian man, medium height, medium weight, clean shaven."

"If we showed you mug shots, do you think you could identify the man?"

"I can try, but he looked very average."

Ahrens turned to Jonathan and Carolyn. All right you're with the Defense Intelligence Agency. Why would this Asian man want to kill you?"

Carolyn said, "He wasn't trying to kill me. I was in my room on the fourth floor."

"So, Mr. Scanlan, why did he want to kill you?"

"I'm not sure. We're part of an investigation. I'm afraid it's classified. I'll give you the name of the man Carolyn, and I report to and his number."

The two detectives were clearly frustrated by Jonathan's answer.

Ahrens stepped forward, crowding Jonathan. "Don't give me some James Bond bullshit. Why did this Asian guy want to kill you?"

Jonathan said nothing. He met the detective's stare until Ahrens backed off. "All right, we're taking you downtown. Maybe that will make you more cooperative."

Jonathan took his cell phone out of his pocket and speed dialed a number. Even though it was quite late in DC, John E Nichols answered on the first ring. In a few words, Jonathan summarized what had happened, listened for a moment, and handed the phone to the detective.

Ahrens began speaking and was abruptly cut off. The rest of his side of the conversation consisted of several, yes sirs.

An obviously pissed off detective handed the phone back to Jonathan. "You need to come down to 100 West 1st Street tomorrow for a formal statement. Our forensic teams will be here soon and this room is a crime scene." Ahrens and Pedder turned and walked out of the room.

Carolyn looked at Myron and Jonathan. "I know what you told the police, and I heard what you said to Director Nichols, but tell me the rest."

Jonathan glanced at his watch. "The bar should still be open and I could use a drink. Let's go downstairs."

CHAPTER 44

Hai Li walked quickly through the lobby and out to his car. Within minutes, he was on the freeway. He knew it was possible that his image had been captured by cameras at the hotel during his stay. If they had his photo, he assumed it would be distributed to all the Southern California airports.

He had earlier received a text regarding Scanlan and the woman's plan to return to San Francisco the following day. He turned onto Highway five and headed north.

He had no intention of informing Beijing about the fiasco at the Marriott. The Shadow could not be known to blow an assassination.

He thought about the failed attempt, but had no idea how Scanlan anticipated the hit. He had to grudgingly admit that the man was smarter than one would think.

———

Jonathan, Carolyn, and Myron were forced to extend their stay for another day in order to provide their statements at police headquarters. Their reception at the facility could only be described as chilly. The veiled threat of a call to the DIA director did keep Detectives Ahrens and Pedder at bay.

Myron left for the six-hour drive to the Bay Area as soon as he retrieved his gun, and they were able to leave the facility. When Jonathan and Carolyn returned to the Sherman Oaks Marriott, they noticed the hotel staff gave them a wide berth. Both felt drained by the prior evening's event. They shared a quiet dinner at the hotel's restaurant.

During dinner, they discussed their next trip to upstate New York and Dallas to dig into the backgrounds of Joyce Galvin and Joseph Wu.

Jonathan did not care which location came first. Carolyn suggested initially going to Wu's contacts in the Dallas area before New York. She wanted to fly down to Washington after they finished looking at Galvin, giving her a couple days to catch up on things at DIA before returning to San Francisco.

Jonathan agreed. "I'll need at least two days to set up the interviews. If you want, you could head back to DC tomorrow and meet me in Dallas when I've lined up the meetings."

"That would be great."

When Jonathan arrived at SFO, Myron was waiting to pick him up. When he stepped out of the Lincoln to load Jonathan's bag in the trunk, he took a moment to glance around.

Myron smiled and said, "I don't see any cartel guys."

Jonathan shook his head, "Not funny."

Right after Jonathan and Myron arrived home, Denise Osmon rang the doorbell with an excited Labrador. Bo nearly knocked Jonathan over as he greeted his master.

Jonathan spent the next three days researching Joyce Galvin and Joseph Wu. Joyce Galvin's background was quite straightforward. She was born and raised in Saratoga Springs, New York, and was valedictorian of her graduating class at Saratoga High School. Joyce then went on to receive her bachelor's degree in Government Studies at Brown.

Joseph Wu's story was more complicated. He was originally from Flower Mound, Texas, and attended the first three years of high school at Marcus High School. A gas explosion killed his parents and destroyed their home. Wu, who had not been at home when his parents were killed, went to live with his aunt and uncle in Frisco, Texas, where he finished high school at Memorial High. He then attended the University of Texas at Austin, graduating in three years with honors.

Jonathan was able to arrange an appointment with Joyce Galvin's parents, who still lived in Saratoga Springs, and her counselor at Brown. He was unable to contact Harriet and Jason Liu, Wu's aunt and uncle. He was able to set up appointments with Ralph Mallen, the principal at Marcus High School, Carol Hamlin Wu's counselor at Memorial High School, as well as with Barbara Gilbert, Wu's counselor at Texas U.

While at home, Jonathan was able to resume running in the Presidio with Bo. This was done after a careful study of the neighborhood by Myron, looking for Asian or Hispanic men. When Jonathan began lining up air and hotel reservations for his trip, Myron insisted on traveling with him.

"Myron, I don't think that will be necessary."

"Don't be ridiculous. Look what happened in Los Angeles."

"Your private investigator's license is for California."

"Yes, but I'm allowed to operate for brief periods in other states. I've already notified the California Bureau of Security and Investigation that I'll be in Texas, New York, and Rhode Island."

"Are you authorized to carry a gun in those states?"

"No problem with Texas. New York and Rhode Island are a little iffy, but I've worked that out." As he said this, he winked at a friend and employer.

Jonatha shook his head but had to admit the trip to Los Angeles would not have worked out well if Myron had not been along. Jonathan picked up his phone and added Myron to his travel plans.

Hai Li received a text with Jonathan's reservations. He made reservations for a flight to Dallas, arriving the day before Scanlan. Jonathan had reserved three rooms at the downtown Marriott. Li considered staying at the same hotel, but decided the risk was too great. The big man had seen him, and while it had been a brief glimpse, there was a chance that he could be recognized.

He booked a room at the nearby Sheraton. He then called Chan

Wening and told him to arrange for a gun to be delivered to his hotel. The head of Intelligence resented being treated like an errand boy and was giving thought to how he could make life difficult for Shadow when all this was over.

CHAPTER 45

On the day before he was scheduled to leave for Dallas, Jonathan called Cal and left a message, suggesting they meet for dinner. Later in the afternoon, Cal called and agreed, asking Jonathan to pick the place. Jonathan told his friend he would pick him up in an Uber at seven.

When Cal slipped into the car, he nodded to Myron, who was in the front passenger seat, and asked, "So, where are we going?"

"The Tadich Grill."

"Great choice. I haven't been there in years."

"I thought I'll probably be eating beef in Texas, so how about a little seafood?"

Myron took a seat at the bar with a view of the front door. Once Jonathan and Cal were settled in a booth with drinks, Cal said, "Close call in Los Angeles."

Jonathan nodded. "As usual, Myron saved my ass."

"Do you think you'll be safe on this trip?"

Jonathan sighed, took a sip of his drink, and said, "I don't know. You know you can only be lucky so many times."

"We can drop this."

"I've thought about it. If this trip doesn't pan out, I'm ready to stop playing DIA agent."

"Any word from Cory?"

Jonathan shook his head, his features somber. "No, I think that ship has sailed. You know, I can't really blame her. She didn't sign up to be shot at."

Cal felt for his friend. He gave Jonathan a smile and asked, "Can this turn into another book?"

The question forced a weak chuckle. "You can't write a book without an ending."

Desperate to lighten the mood, Cal asked, "How has Carolyn worked out?"

"Actually, quite well. She's very smart and has handled herself well. You know, she was asking about you."

Cal sat back and gave his friend a puzzled look. "What do you mean?"

"You know, personal stuff, like are you in a relationship, were you ever married, stuff like that."

"Really?" Jonathan could not tell if Cal was pleased or frightened.

"Yeah, I think she's interested in you."

Cal was not sure how to respond. Instead, he picked up the menu and said, "We'd better order."

The balance of the evening's discussion focused on the 49er's key injuries and whether the team could make the playoffs.

Denise Osmon picked up Bo before Jonathan and Myron left for the airport. Their flight was slightly delayed, but they managed to arrive at their hotel in the early evening. Carolyn had already checked in and was waiting for them in the lobby.

After Jonathan and Myron checked in and dropped their bags off in their rooms, they joined Carolyn at the hotel's main restaurant. Jonathan was somewhat bothered by their inability to locate Wu's aunt and uncle. They had apparently moved out of their rental when their nephew went to the University of Texas. Their driver's licenses had expired and had not been renewed by the state.

When they were seated, Jonathan ordered a glass of Chardonnay, Myron a beer, and Carolyn a club soda with a lime. Jonathan thought about asking her about the club soda, but then thought better of it. Over dinner, they talked about the upcoming interviews. Flower Mound was thirty-seven miles northwest of Dallas, and Frisco was thirty-five miles south of the city.

Jonathan had scheduled the appointment at Marcus High at ten in the morning and Memorial High School in Frisco at three in the afternoon. The following day, they were scheduled to make the short flight to Austin.

Hai Li had watched Jonathan and Myron arrive at the Marriott but stayed well out of sight. He did not think the big man would recognize him, but he was not sure. He saw no opportunity to kill them while they were in the hotel, but he was confident there would be an opening soon.

Myron had rented a Ford Explorer for the day, and Carolyn programmed the SUV's navigation system to guide them to Flower Mound and the high school. Traffic was slow as they worked their way across Dallas, but they had allowed plenty of time to make the short trip.

Myron remained in the Ford when they reached the school. Ralph Mallen, the school's principal, was a short, energetic man, somewhere in his fifties. When Jonathan and Carolyn came to his office, he bounced out of his chair to greet them. He vigorously pumped their hands before offering them his visitor's chairs.

"My, the Defense Intelligence Agency. How exciting. How can I help you?"

Carolyn took the lead. "We're updating the backgrounds of Pentagon employees who handle highly classified information. Do you recall a student named Joseph Wu?"

"I didn't know the young man well. What happened to his parents was certainly a tragedy."

"Was he a good student?"

"I'm not sure. Let me go get his student records."

The principal left the office for several minutes. When he returned, he was holding a printout. "He was a B average student. I do recall that he was a very good athlete. He was the best receiver on our football team."

"Any other outside activities or interests, like the debating team or school politics?"

This drew a blank expression. "Not that I recall, but like I said, I didn't know the young man very well."

"Did he have any close friends we can talk to?"

"I'm sorry, I wouldn't know."

They thanked the man and left the school. With a good deal of time to kill before their three o'clock appointment, they returned to their hotel. They failed to notice the silver Toyota Corolla that followed them, staying several cars back.

On returning to the Marriott, they had a quick lunch, then went to their rooms to make a few calls. At two, they set off for Frisco and Memorial High School. When they reached the school, they were directed to Carol Hamlin's office, the woman who had been Wu's counselor. Carol Hamlin turned out to be a friendly, overweight middle-aged woman.

Carolyn again took the lead. After the initial introductions and the explanation that their visit related to Joseph Wu's security clearance, Ms. Hamlin was quite expansive about Joseph Wu's academic record.

"Joseph was an exceptional student. I believe he received straight As during his year with us."

This caused Carolyn and Jonathan to share a glance. Jonathan gave a confused look at the counselor. "We visited Marcus High School in Flower Mound. Joseph Wu was a B student during his first three years."

"I don't know what else I can tell you. Joseph was a brilliant student."

"We understand he played football at his prior school. Was he on the team when he was here?"

Hamlin shook her head. "I don't believe he was."

Carolyn asked, "Was he involved in any other activities?"

The woman shook her head. "Not that I'm aware of."

"Did he have any close friends we can contact?"

"I'm sorry. I wouldn't know."

On the way back to the hotel, Jonathan turned to Carolyn. "Quite a change. A slightly better than average student to an exceptional one."

"Maybe the death of his parents had an impact."

"Maybe."

CHAPTER 46

The three-hour flight to Austin was uneventful. Myron rented a car at Hertz for the ride to the university. Myron remained in the car as Carolyn and Jonathan walked into the campus. After several wrong turns, they found the LBJ School of Public Affairs and Barbara Gilbert's office.

Ms. Gilbert had been Joseph's counselor. She was a tall, rail-thin woman with steel gray hair worn at shoulder length. She smiled in greeting and motioned them into the visitor's chairs facing her desk.

"I understand your visit is about Joseph Wu."

Carolyn explained about updating the man's background related to his security clearance. The counselor opened a file on her desk. "I'm not sure what you want to know. Joseph was a brilliant student. He graduated with honors with a bachelor's degree in public affairs."

Jonathan asked, "Can you describe his personality?"

Barbara Girbert pushed back in her chair and gave the question some thought. "Joseph was somewhat shy. I found him to be a pleasant young man, but not particularly outgoing."

"He was apparently quite an athlete in high school."

This comment brought a smile. "Really, I never would have guessed."

"So, he didn't play wide receiver for the Longhorns."

Gilbert laughed. "No. A great student, but nothing outside of academics."

"Did he have any close friends we can contact?"

"As I said, Joseph is somewhat shy. I don't know if he had any close friends."

They thanked the counselor and walked back to their car. When they got it, Myron said, "We may have been followed. There was a dark blue sedan, I think a Honda, that pulled into the lot just after we got here. I believe I noticed it on the drive from the airport. No one got out of the car after it parked."

Jonathan glanced at Myron. "Well, let's see what happens next. We're booked in at the Hilton at the airport."

Shortly after they left the university parking lot, the blue Honda followed, staying several cars behind them.

Carolyn tensed up. "Do you think they'll attack us?"

Jonathan shook his head. "No. They must know Myron's armed."

Hai Li stayed well back from Myron's Ford SUV. He had information regarding the airline reservations Jonathan, Carolyn, and Myron would be taking the next day, but his people had not been able to give him anything on the hotel they would be staying at this evening.

Once he saw them turn into the Hilton at the Austin airport, he turned away.

The trip to Dallas and Austin had increased Beijing's demands to eliminate Scanlan and his friends, as it was apparent they were focusing on Joseph Wu. Li did not believe he could successfully hit Scanlan while he was at the Hilton.

He had sent Chan Wening a text, demanding high-quality help to take out Scanlan in New York.

Myron dropped Jonathan and Carolyn off at the hotel before driving the rental to Hertz and turning it in. Jonathan had made dinner reservations at Creeks Restaurant at the hotel. After checking in, he went to his room and called Cal, leaving a message describing what they had learned about

Wu. The dinner reservation was at seven, but with nothing more to do, he went down to the restaurant twenty minutes early and ordered a drink at the bar.

Carolyn was the first to join him. Once she was settled in with her club soda, Jonathan asked her, "Any conclusions about Mr. Wu?"

"No, the transition from being a B student and a football player to a shy, outstanding student is puzzling."

Jonathan nodded in agreement. "Like you said, maybe losing his parents the way he did could explain it, but it is odd."

When Myron arrived and joined them at their table. Jonathan turned to Myron. "See any Asian men lurking around the hotel?"

"No, but when you go to your room, lock the door and, if someone knocks, don't open it unless it's Carolyn or me."

The hotel's restaurant had a limited menu, but they each found something to order. Jonathan did find a decent Chardonnay. While they were waiting for their orders, Carolyn asked, "What's the game plan for New York?"

"Given our arrival time at JFK and the one-hour time difference, I booked us into the Hyatt Regency at the airport. The next day, we have an appointment with Joyce Gavin's parents in Saratoga Springs and with her guidance counselor at her high school. The next day, we'll drive to Brown University and talk to her counselor there. It's about a three-hour drive from New York to Saratoga Springs and another three hours to get to Brown in Rhode Island. So, I made hotel reservations for one night in Saratoga Springs and one night in Providence."

Myron asked, "And then we all go home?"

"I guess, unless something pops up."

CHAPTER 47

Their midday flight into the John F Kennedy airport put them into their hotel in the early afternoon. Once checked in, they went their separate ways, agreeing to meet for dinner at seven. Jonathan used his free time to work out at the hotel's gym while Carolyn spent time on the phone briefing the DIA director.

Myron went to Enterprise and picked up a Jeep Cherokee in the morning for their trip north. After fighting through the congestion at the airport, they made their way north on the I-87.

———

Hai Li's people shadowed the three from the airport terminal to their hotel. In the morning, two cars followed Myron, Carolyn, and Jonathan out of the city and north toward Saratoga Springs. Hai Li was driving a silver Toyota Camry, and three of his men were in a black Nissan Rogue. Both cars stayed well back from Myron's Jeep, alternating positions to avoid detection.

Nothing happened until the three cars had passed the exits for Albany. Traffic had thinned, and the countryside had become more rural. The Nissan Rogue moved up, pulling alongside the Jeep in the left lane.

The windows on the passenger side were lowered, and men at each window extended weapons.

Myron slammed on the brakes, quickly dropping back behind the Rogue. Carolyn screamed at Myron, "Give me your gun."

Myron, realizing he could not drive and shoot, handed her his Glock. The Nissan SUV had slowed as it tried to drop back alongside the Jeep. Carolyn, who was seated in the back of the Jeep, lowered her window.

She shouted at Myron to hit the gas. As they passed the Nissan, Carolyn began firing at the vehicle. The Rogue veered sharply to the left, hit the divider, and then spun across the freeway, rolling over as it left the road.

No one in the Jeep said a word as Carolyn rolled up her window. She picked up her phone, first calling 911 to report the *accident,* then calling Director Nichols to report what had just happened.

Myron, who had not stopped at the scene, glanced back at Carolyn and said, "You're my type of girl."

Carolyn smiled as she handed him back his gun.

They did not notice the silver Toyota Camry that had fallen back, but had also not stopped to offer aid.

When they reached the exit for Saratoga Springs, they followed the navigation system's directions to Cady Hill Boulevard. The Galvin's home was a stately, two-story white colonial with black shutters and a black roof. Not a mansion, but quite nice.

Jonathan had not spoken a word since the shooting and turned to Carolyn as they walked to the front door. "You take the lead, please."

Joyce's father answered the door, introducing himself as Seth Galvin. He was a man of medium height, somewhere in his fifties, with short hair, starting to gray. He smiled as he ushered Jonathan and Carolyn into his home.

His wife appeared, smiling. Seth said, "My wife, Kathleen." He led them into the living room and asked if they would like coffee or water. Jonathan and Carolyn declined and took seats on a sofa. Carolyn gave the background check story and began asking questions about Joyce.

Both Kathleen and Seth were obviously proud of their daughter and described her achievements in glowing terms. After half an hour, Carolyn and Jonathan thanked them for agreeing to meet with them and left the home.

The Saratoga High School was a short drive from the Galvin's home. They met with Patricia Eckert, Joyce's counselor. The woman explained that she had only known Joyce during her senior year, as the student's previous counselor had retired.

"Joyce was a highly intelligent student. Not quite straight As, but close. I believe she went on to Brown."

"Yes, and did quite well there, as well. What was she like as a person?"

The counselor gave Carolyn a questioning look. "What do you mean?"

"Was she shy or outgoing? Did she have a lot of close friends? Participate in outside activities?"

Patricia Eckert shrugged. "I don't know. She was a normal, pleasant teenager."

Seeing no further progress in sight, they thanked the woman and left.

Myron drove them to the Saratoga Hilton. After checking in they agreed to meet at the hotel bar at six. When Jonathan called Cal, the computer wizard was stunned when his friend described the woman who was interested in him as Rambo in a skirt.

Jonathan had made reservations at the hotel restaurant, called The Springs. Once he, Carolyn, and Myron were seated, with drinks on the way, he turned to Carolyn. "I can't believe what you did. How did you learn to shoot like that?"

Carolyn shrugged. "It's part of our training. All the agents that work in the field have to be trained and qualify annually."

"But you're not carrying."

"I didn't think I needed to on these interviews. I obviously was wrong. I'm having a weapon delivered to my room tonight."

Myron smiled at the woman. "I don't think the boys in that SUV will be after us tomorrow."

"No, I talked to Director Nichols. Two of them are dead, and one is in intensive care, all Asians with no IDs. By the way, he cleared it all with the locals, so we don't have to spend time answering questions."

Jonathan noticed Carolyn had ordered a gin and tonic. She smiled when she noticed his interest. "I don't normally drink on duty, but I thought tonight could be the exception."

Both men toasted her with their drinks.

CHAPTER 48

The morning drive to Providence took three hours, but was remarkably uneventful when compared to the trip to Saratoga Springs. They found Brown University without a problem and, after a few wrong turns, Carolyn and Jonahan arrived at Frederick Jorge's office. When they knocked on the counselor's door, a high-pitched voice invited them in.

Fredrick Jorge was a tall, thin man in his sixties. He had a narrow face, dominated by bushy eyebrows and thick horned rimmed glasses. When he rose from his desk to greet his visitors, his long body seemed to be unfolding.

"Mr. Scanlan and Ms. Staten?"

Jonathan stepped up and shook the man's hand. "Jonathan and Carolyn."

"And please call me Fred."

After explaining the purpose of their visit, they settled into the counselor's visitor chairs. The counselor asked, "So, what do you want to know about Joyce Galvin?"

"We understand she did well academically. How would you describe her personality?"

The question seemed to take the counselor by surprise. After a moment, he said, "Joyce was a pretty normal student, personality-wise. I only had limited contact with her, but she was pleasant and quite bright, perhaps a little on the quiet side."

"Did she participate in any outside activities, sports, debate club, things like that?"

"No sports. I don't know of anything else."

"Do you know any of Joyce's close friends?

"I have no idea regarding her friends."

Fifteen minutes more of probing yielded nothing of interest.

They thanked Mr. Jorge, left the office, and walked back to Myron and their car. Carolyn shook her head as she slid into the back seat. "Not much there."

Jonathan nodded in agreement. "Pretty much what you'd expect. Let's head back to the big apple."

Traffic was heavy on I-95 as they made their way past New Haven, Stamford and White Plains. It was after six when they pulled into the Hyatt Regency. Myron turned in the rental as Jonathan and Carolyn checked in at the reception desk.

Hai Li had followed them at a discreet distance. After the attempt on the way to Saratoga Springs, he had no intention to try to take them out on the road. The text messages from Chan Wening were increasingly demanding, reflecting pressure from Beijing.

He thought about taking a room at the Hyatt, but decided the risk was too great. He called and made a one-night reservation at the nearby Residence Inn. After checking in, he took a cab to the Hyatt and walked through the lobby to the Sugar Factory American Brasserie restaurant.

Given the time of their arrival, he was fairly sure they would be using the restaurant for dinner. While attacking them in the restaurant would be relatively easy, escaping the hotel would be nearly impossible. He had no desire to spend the rest of his life in a New York prison.

He also had no information on Scanlan's room number; he knew the hotel would not provide that information. He decided to wait for Scanlan and his friends to finish dinner and then follow the man as he went to his room. A quick shot when the man was in the elevator or in the hallway would eliminate the threat to Beijing.

His immediate problem was locating a place where he could keep track of Scanlan while he was at dinner without being obvious. The restaurant was in a large open room, offering nowhere for him to sit without being visible. The same situation existed for the lobby.

Hai Li knew he could not stand around the lobby for over an hour without drawing attention to himself. He glanced at his watch. It was almost seven. He had to assume Scanlan and his two companions would be showing up any time for dinner. Dinner would probably take somewhat over an hour. He left the hotel and walked away from the entrance, planning to return a little after eight. On the way out of the hotel, he noticed a newspaper a guest had left on a table. He picked it up, planning to pretend to be reading it when he came back.

Just after eight, he returned and took a seat in the lobby and used the newspaper to cover his features. He did not have to wait long, as at 8:15, Scanlan, the woman, and the big man walked from the restaurant to the elevators.

Hai Li walked quickly to the stairs and ran up to the second floor. He opened the door to the second floor and watched the woman step out of the elevator and begin walking down the hallway.

He then raced up to the third floor, opened the door, but no one had left the elevator. He then ran up the stairs to the fourth floor. This time he watched Scanlan and the big man leave the elevator and walk down the hall to their rooms.

Scanlan inserted his plastic card and entered his room. The big man opened the door to the adjacent room. The same arrangement they had used at the Marriott Courtyard in Sherman Oaks.

Hai Li knew Jonathan Scanlan was not a stupid man. He also remembered how his *knock on the door* idea had fared in Southern California. After staring at Scanlan's door for a moment, he decided the idea was a poor one. He left the hotel and returned to the Residence Inn.

CHAPTER 49

The following morning, Jonathan, Carolyn, and Myron returned to JFK. Carolyn was taking a short hop to DC, while Jonathan and Myron had reservations on a United flight to San Francisco. Neither Carolyn nor Jonathan was a happy camper. Other than not getting shot, they had little to show for their cross-country exploits.

In addition to the lack of progress toward uncovering the source of the leaks, the threat to Jonathan, Cal, and possibly Cory was still real. It seemed like Myron, Jim Stack, and Lamar Williams had found permanent employment. For Jonathan, the cost of the men protecting Cory, Cal, and himself was insignificant. What he hated was the impact on his personal life. He could not go running, play golf, or hit balls at the driving range without concerns about being shot. He assumed the same problem was bothering Cory and Cal.

Two days after his return to the city, a video conference call had been arranged between Director Nichols, Cal, Carolyn, and Jonathan. Jonathan joined Cal at his condominium for the end of the conference.

After the preliminary processes were completed, assuring everyone was online, Director Nichols took the lead. "Well, I'm just glad everyone is back safe and sound. Our opposition seems to be pulling out all the stops. I'm very proud of how you all handled yourselves."

Jonathan's expression was grim as he faced the screen. "I appreciate your comment, but, frankly, I don't think we've moved the needle much in locating the leaker, and I believe they're going to keep trying."

"Unfortunately, I believe you're right. Cal, have you come up with anything?"

"No sir. I've taken a deep dive into the three people we focused on, and I can find no trace of any money being received."

"Could payments be going to offshore accounts, like the Caymans?"

"It's possible, but if so, based on their spending and account balances, the funds were never touched."

"We've also spent a great deal of time looking at the three young people, and we've come up with nothing. They all seem to be bright, good Americans."

Cal said, "I've also spent time checking out their social media activity. Joyce uses Meta, but neither Carlos Bourdet nor Joseph Wu shows any social media activity."

Cal and Jonathan watched Director Nichols shake his head in frustration. "Perhaps we were premature in narrowing it down to these three people."

Jonathan and Cal nodded. Cal said, "The original list included twenty people. If we exclude Galvin, Bourdet, and Wu, we'll be looking at seventeen people."

Carolyn spoke up for the first time. "Wouldn't someone have to have a good deal of training before they could operate as a spy?"

No one spoke for a minute as they considered her question. Nichols broke the silence. "I'm not sure a great deal of training would be required to pass on classified information, but, yes, some training would be required."

Jonathan commented, "I assume the people doing the training would be Chinese. Wouldn't it raise a red flag if this person were seen hanging out with Chinese agents?"

Nichols nodded. "So, it would make sense for the soon-to-be leaker to go somewhere secure for this training."

Cal jumped in. "Let's take a look and see if any of the people on the list had an unusual absence from school or work. That would mean a trip without friends or family."

Carolyn asked, "How can we figure out that type of information?"

Cal said, "Hopefully, they used a credit card."

There was a long pause before Nichols spoke. "It's worth a try."

When the video conference ended, Cal turned to Jonathan. "This is going to take time."

Jonathan thought for a moment. "I think we can limit the time period to the interval between when the person started working for the government and when DIA became aware of the leaks."

"That helps somewhat, but we're still talking about seventeen people."

"No, look at all twenty."

Cal gave a hollow laugh. "Thanks, buddy."

CHAPTER 50

While Cal toiled through years of credit card records, Jonathan returned to his somewhat normal routines. He ran in the Presidio with Bo and hit balls at the driving range. The difference was the omnipresence of Myron, watching his back.

The only break from Cal and Jonathan's limited activities was poker night at Cal's condo with the Pacific Avenue Irregulars. It had been months since their last gathering, and everyone wanted to catch up on Cal and Jonathan's most recent adventures.

Cal explained that so far, they had not been able to pin down the leaker, but they were still looking at the aides and staffers. He decided not to mention their adventures in Southern California and New York.

Jonathan enjoyed the evening for the brief period of normality it provided.

The following week, Jonathan was at his desk paying bills when his phone chirped. A glance at the screen showed his father's name. While he was close to his parents, phone calls were rare. Jonathan's initial reaction was fear that one of his parents had a health issue. He was relieved when he heard his father's cheerful voice.

"Jonathan, we haven't talked to you for a while. How is everything going?"

"Everything's fine. How about you and mom?"

"We're good. We were talking about flying up to see you and your new house."

"Love to have you, but I'm still involved in this investigation and I'm going to have to be traveling again fairly soon. Can we put the visit off for a bit?"

"Sure. How's Cory?"

"Dad, I'm afraid that doesn't seem to be working out."

There was silence for a moment. "We're sorry. We were hoping she was the one."

"I know."

"If you're going to be traveling, what about Bo?"

"I have a woman who takes him into her home when I'm away."

While what he told his father was true, the real reason he put off his parents' planned visit was having to explain why he had to have armed protection and that people were trying to kill him. He wondered if that would ever change.

The following week Cal called and suggested a meeting. "Have you been able to come up with anything?"

"Maybe. No smoking gun, but we need to talk. I'll line up a conference call with Carolyn. When can you get here?"

"I can get there in twenty minutes."

"Give me a little more time to line up, Carolyn. How about two hours?"

"Sure." Jonathan's mood immediately perked up. If Cal could identify the leaker, perhaps this nightmare could end.

It was still early enough in the day for street parking to be available when Jonathan pulled up to Cal's condominium. Myron and Jonathan were buzzed in and greeted at the door. Cal herded Jonathan to his desk and pointed to his computer screen.

"I lined up a video conference with Carolyn. The director wasn't available."

Cal sat at his desk and opened the video. Carolyn's face appeared with a hopeful expression. After a few brief pleasantries, he began describing the process he followed. Jonathan became increasingly anxious and frustrated. He wanted to know the time, not how to make a watch.

Eventually, the normally stoic Carolyn interrupted Cal's monologue. "Cal, please cut to the chase."

This momentarily threw Cal off stride, but he quickly recovered. "Okay. Virtually all the people on the list took trips during the time frame between when they took jobs at the Pentagon and when the leaks started. I was able to identify some as work-related or trips to see their family. There were obvious vacation trips. If they were traveling with friends or family, these could be eliminated. Eleven are married, and they traveled with their spouse on all their non-work-related trips. Four of the single employees took trips that were with friends. One, interestingly enough, took no trips that were not work-related. That was Joseph Wu. If we accept this as a valid criterion, we're down to four people."

Jonathan and Carolyn studied the four remaining on the list. Jonathan said, "Refresh my memory. What do we know about them?"

Cal shuffled through another folder on his desk. "Marie Grande, twenty-six, is from Doylestown, which is just outside Philadelphia. She has a bachelor's from Georgetown and reports to Colonel Handy. Stephen Stone is thirty, grew up in Long Beach, and went to USC. He reports to General Kelly. John Berman is twenty-four. He's from Seattle, graduated from Washington State, and reports to General Farrell. Robert Frey is twenty-nine, from Evanston, and stayed home, graduating from Northwestern. He also reports to General Farrell."

Carolyn asked, "What were the trips these four took that rang a bell?"

Cal picked up his notes. "Grande spent ten days in Minot, North Dakota, in November, two years ago. Stone went to Albuquerque, New Mexico, for nine days in October three years ago. Borman spent a week in Henderson, Nevada, in July three years ago, and Frey went to Jackson, Mississippi, in August for eight days. And keep in mind, the brief that triggered the Chinese reaction went to Handy, Farrell, and Kelly."

Carolyn and Jonathan waited for more. "Of course, there could be innocent explanations, but who would want to spend ten days in Minot in November? What about Henderson in July or Mississippi in August?

Albuquerque in October might be all right, but what do you do in Albuquerque for nine days?"

After thinking about it for a moment, Carolyn and Jonathan had to agree that these were valid questions. Cal broke into their thoughts when he asked, "So, what happens next?"

Carolyn said, "Well, since I'm here and the four people are here, I could question them."

"Should I come out?"

"No, Jonathan. I can question them at work. If their explanations don't make sense, you can come out for the second round."

"Great. How long will it take?"

"Unless one or more are unavailable for some reason, I'd say two days."

Cal and Jonathan sat back after Carolyn went offline. Jonathan sighed as he looked at his friend. "I hope this leads us somewhere. I'm tired of living like this."

"I know. I like Lamar, but it feels like this has been going on forever."

When Jonathan left Cal's condo, he held a faint hope that Carolyn might be able to provide an end to their investigation.

CHAPTER 51

Two days later, Carolyn called, and a hasty telephone conference was set up. Jonathan had to use his cell phone, since he believed the tap on his landline was still in place.

"I interviewed all four people. We can look at them further, but I believe we can scratch three off the list. Marie Grande was in Minot to see her boyfriend, Wilson Stanton, who's a pilot at the Minot Air Force Base. Stephen Stone was in Albuquerque for a hot air ballon event that ran from October 3rd to the 11th. John Berman was staying with a buddy named Billy Tosetti in Henderson. Basically, they were partying it up in next door Las Vegas."

"So, that leaves Robert Frey."

"Yes. My impression is that he was evasive. When I pressed him, he said he just wanted to see the south. I'm pretty good at reading people, and my bullshit meter was going off."

Cal jumped right in. "Okay, I'll zero in on Frey."

Jonathan asked, "Do you think pressing him harder would get us anywhere?"

Carolyn took a moment to answer. "Maybe, but I don't think so."

"Well, why don't you and I visit Jackson, Mississippi? We can trace his movements from his credit card receipts, and maybe Cal can get a hold of his phone records."

"Sure, when do you want to head south?"

"How about in three days. That should give Cal a little time to dig around."

"Fine, I'll text you my flight information. Director Nichols wants one of our agents to join us. His name is Douglas Hillman, and he's based at our facility in Huntsville, Alabama."

"Is that really necessary?"

"After the attack in upstate New York, he believes it is. Hilman will be driving from Huntsville, and he'll make his own reservation when I know where we'll be staying."

"I'll make the hotel reservations and let you know."

Jonathan booked two rooms at the Weston Jackson, the hotel Frey had stayed at. Myron pressed to accompany Jonathan, but Jonathan did not think it would be necessary, as Carolyn and Hillman would be armed.

There were no direct flights to Jackson, forcing Jonathan to go through O'Hare and Carolyn through Atlanta.

As soon as Jonathan made the reservations, Hai Li received the information. He arranged to fly to Jackson one day before Jonathan and, this time he booked a room at Scanlan's hotel. He also arranged for a weapon to be delivered when he arrived. Neither he nor Beijing had any idea why Jonathan Scanlan would be flying to Jackson, Mississippi, but both viewed it as another opportunity to take the man out.

With the time change and the change of planes in Chicago, it was early evening before Jonathan arrived at his hotel. While Carolyn had the advantage of a one-hour time change, it was still a long day. When Jonathan checked in at the Weston, he found Carolyn had already arrived. He called her room, and they agreed to meet for dinner at the hotel's Estelle Southern Table.

Jonathan was pleased to see the restaurant had a well-stocked wine bar. He was halfway through his glass of Chardonnay when Carolyn joined him. Both were somewhat drained from their long travel day.

When Carolyn joined him, she ordered a gin and tonic. When

Jonathan raised his eyebrows in mock surprise, she said, "I think you're a bad influence. By the way, Hillman will be coming in later this evening."

Jonathan had to smile. "Have you spent much time in the south?"

"Not much. I was involved in a case in Louisiana. That's about it."

"I never asked, where are you from originally?"

"I grew up in Charlotte, North Carolina. How about you?"

"Walnut Creek. It's a suburb in the Bay Area."

"Parents still there?"

"No, they moved to St. George, Utah, several years ago. Let's get a table."

Once seated with menus, Jonathan quickly settled on the little gem salad and a medium-rare grilled Hartford filet. Carolyn had trouble deciding. At the waiter's suggestion, she went with the gem salad and the blackened red fish.

Neither noticed the middle-aged Asian man seated at a table on the other side of the restaurant. He could not hear their conversation, but he was sure the woman had been with Scanlan in Los Angeles and New York. He assumed she would be armed, but his misogynistic beliefs discounted her as a serious threat.

Hai Li tried to time the signing of his check in sync with when Scanlan and the woman finished dinner. The waiter was busy with other diners and did not reach his table until Jonathan and Carolyn had walked out of the restaurant. When it was presented, he quickly signed his check and hurried out of the restaurant. The door of the elevator containing Jonathan, Carolyn and two other guests closed as Hai Li crossed the lobby.

It took him several minutes to locate the stairs. When he ran up to the second floor, it was apparent that the elevators at the Westin were quite fast and there was no way he could reach Scanlan's floor before the man was in his room.

Frustrated, the man they called Shadow, went to his room and considered his options.

CHAPTER 52

Jonathan was back at the hotel's café having coffee when Carolyn arrived the following morning. She had just ordered her coffee when a man approached their table. "Mr. Scanlan and Agent Staten?"

Both Jonathan and Carolyn nodded. "Douglas Hillman." The DIA agent had the former military look: close-cropped blond hair, trim athletic build, and an erect posture.

After a round of handshaking, Hillman sat down and ordered coffee and a glass of orange juice. Jonathan smiled, "It's Carolyn and Jonathan."

Hillman returned the smile. "Please call me Doug."

"Have you been briefed on what we're doing?"

Doug nodded. "Only the basics. You're trying to identify the person at the Pentagon leaking classified information."

Carolyn nodded. "Yes. We believe the intel is going to the CCP. We're going on the assumption that the person doing the leaking had to receive training, so we're looking at people that had access to the classified information and went somewhere for their training. One of the people we're looking at spent eight days here in Jackson three years ago in August. When I questioned the man in DC, he didn't give me a good answer for the trip."

Doug Hillman sat back and absorbed what Carolyn had said. "Okay, sounds like this guy is a maybe, but why did they send me here?"

Carolyn nodded. "Since we started the investigation there have been four attempts to kill Jonathan. I was with him on the last try."

"So, I'm here to protect you." This said in a calm, noncommittal tone.

"Are you okay with that?"

"Sure, but aren't you armed?"

"I am, Jonathan's not."

Doug glanced at Jonathan with a puzzled expression. "Why not?"

"I'm not a regular agent. I was brought in because I'm pretty good at solving puzzles."

This seemed to satisfy Doug. "All right, how do you plan to solve this puzzle?"

"The guy we're looking at is named Robert Frey. We have his credit card and phone records. We'll see who he talked to, and who he spent time with. Hopefully some of the places he went will have him on security video."

"Okay, where do we start?"

"Right here. He stayed at this hotel and ate at two of the restaurants. The head of security is meeting with us in thirty minutes."

When they finished their coffee, they went to the front desk. Jonathan explained to the clerk that they were meeting with Michael Phillips. The clerk motioned to one of the bell hops and asked the young man to take them to the security office.

Michael Phippips turned out to be an affable black man of about fifty, with a shiny Michael Jordan shaved head. All three offered their credentials. Jonathan pulled a sheet out of a folder.

"We'd like to review your security tapes for two of your restaurants. The Iron Horse Grill on August 3^{rd,} 2020, and for Estelle Southern Table on August 5th, the same year."

Phillips smiled broadly and shook his head. "We'd like to help, but we only save tapes for three years."

They thanked the head of hotel security and were about to leave when Hillman asked, "Mr. Phillips, what do you do with the tapes that have been replaced?"

Phillips had a blank expression for a moment, then said, "I don't know. Hang on a minute." He picked up his phone and dialed an extension. After a brief conversation, he hung up and turned back to Doug. "We use an outside company to maintain our video equipment. They replace the tapes. They're a local company named Beats Electronics."

Phillips scribbled on a note pad and handed it to Jonathan. "This is their phone number. The owner is Harrison Beats."

When they were out of Phillips office, Jonathan dialed the number he had been given. The woman that answered told him that Harrison Beats was out of the office, but should be returning at about three.

Jonathan relayed this to Carolyn and Doug, and said, "Let's try a few of the other places where Frey used his credit card. Maybe we'll have more luck at one of them."

As they piled into Doug's Ford Explorer, they did not notice the Asian man walking to his Honda CR-V. They followed the navigation prompts to La Presa Taqueria. It was too early for the lunch crowd and the restaurant was empty of customers. A man and a woman were busy behind the counter.

The man looked up and said, "Sorry, folks, we don't open for another hour."

Carolyn stepped forward. "That's okay, we're not here for lunch." She showed the man her credentials.

"The Defense Intelligence Agency, really?"

"Yes, really. Do you have video cameras covering the restaurant?"

The man paused for a moment. "Yeah, one covers the register, and another covers the seating area."

"We want the tapes from August 4th, 2020."

The man laughed, "Man, that's over five years ago. We only keep tapes for six months."

"What do you do with the old tapes?"

He shrugged. "Throw them away, I guess."

———

Hai Li sat in his car, watching Scanlan and his two companions as they left the taqueria. He was sure the woman and the newly arrived man would be armed. The odds of him surviving a shootout on the streets were not favorable. He did not care about the woman or the new man and believed that at some point, Scanlan would be careless. When they returned to their hotel, they each went to their rooms to make phone calls. They agreed to meet in the lobby at 2:30. Jonathan spent some time studying the list of Frey's credit card records. Some of the restaurant charges were quite high, indicating he paid for two dinners. He thought this was odd. If you are here being trained by your Chinese handler, wouldn't the handler be picking up the tab?

The drive to Beats Electronics did not take long. When they arrived, the woman at a desk in the entry glanced at their credentials and waved them into the owner's office.

"Mr. Beats, we're from the Defense Intelligence Agency and have some questions about the security tapes from the restaurants at the Weston."

Harrison Beats came around his desk to greet his guests. "Sure, can I see your credentials?"

"Of course." They each offered their credentials. Carolyn asked, "How far back do you keep the tapes?"

Beats shrugged and scratched the top of his balding head. "I don't know. There's no set time."

"We're looking for the evening tapes for the Iron House on August 3rd, 2020, and the Estelle in the evening of August 5th, the same year."

Beats went around his desk, took out a pad, and wrote down the dates. "This is going to take a little while. Why don't you go down the street to Starbucks and come back in an hour?"

They thanked the man and followed his advice. When they returned, the woman at the desk smiled and pointed to two tapes. "Here they are."

Carolyn suggested they could make copies and return the originals. "Don't bother. Nobody's going to want five-year-old tapes."

Carolyn gave the woman her card. "Call me if you need them back."

They returned to the Weston, marched through the lobby and knocked on Michael Phillips's door. When he opened the door Jonathan asked if they could use his facility to review the tapes.

He agreed and led them down the hall to a backroom. Phillips loaded one of the tapes and showed them how to operate the system. "When you've finished watching this one, come back to my office, and I'll set up the other one."

The first tape was for the Iron Horse, and they were able to fast-forward to 6:00 PM. Carolyn stopped the tape when a dark-haired man came into view. "That's Frey."

They spent over an hour watching the man eat dinner by himself. After Phillips loaded the tape for the Estelle restaurant, the process was repeated. Again, the man ate dinner alone.

They thanked Phillips and returned to the lobby. Jonathan turned to Doug and Carolyn. "Jesus, we just spent a day so we could watch this guy eat dinner. Come on, I'm buying."

CHAPTER 53

The information provided by Cal included a list of telephone numbers Robert Frey had called over the prior six months. The majority of the numbers had been researched and eliminated as not relevant. One number stood out: 601 555-1200. The number belonged to NAI UCR, a large real estate firm that handled the brokerage and management for commercial and residential properties in Jackson. Unfortunately, there was no way to trace the calls to an individual at the firm.

While significant, Jonathan found it difficult to see how he could use the information. One of the larger charges on Frey's credit card was to a nightclub called Club Anonymous. Jonathan googled the address. While Jonathan did not frequent nightclubs, he did know no one would be there until later that evening.

During the day, Jonathan, Carolyn, and Doug visited three retail stores where Frey had made purchases. Two did not have video security systems, and the one that did, laughed when asked if they had tapes from five years ago. After dinner at Drago's Seafood Restaurant, the three drove to the nightclub. The parking lot outside the club was almost full. When they reached the entrance, the bouncer told them there was a twenty-dollar cover charge. They flashed their credentials and told him they were not here as customers. At first, the man was not sure what to do, but finally let them inside.

The place was what they expected to see: dim lighting, loud music, and men and women dancing. What differentiated Club Anonymous was that the men were dancing with men and the women were dancing with women. Clearly, the club was a gay bar.

They approached the bar and asked to see the manager. A tall, thin man dressed all in black appeared. They presented their credentials and asked about the club's video cameras.

The man stared at them for an angry moment. "Do you have a subpoena?"

When Jonathan shook his head, the manager told him to fuck off, turned and walked away.

On the way back to the hotel, Carolyn said, "That went well. Are we going to have to come up with a subpoena?"

Jonathan thought for a moment. "Maybe. I can't see Frey and his Chinese handler going to a gay nightclub. This isn't adding up. Last night I was looking at Frey's credit card charges. On at least two occasions, he paid for two dinners. If he was meeting with a CCP handler, why would he be paying the bill?"

No one had an answer.

Hai Li followed them to the nightclub and back to the hotel. The communications he was receiving from Chan Wening and Beijing were more and more demanding, even bordering on threatening.

When they returned to the hotel, they each returned to their room. Jonathan turned on the television, but found nothing he wanted to watch. He was pacing in the small confines of his room when he decided to go downstairs for a drink.

He took a seat at the wine bar at Estelle's Southern Table and ordered a glass of Chardonnay. Most of the dinner crowd had left, with only a few tables still occupied. Jonathan was the only patron at the wine bar.

Hai Li was feeling the pressure from Beijing and was walking through the lobby when he glanced into the restaurant and saw Scanlan sitting alone. He quickly went to his room, packed his bag, and took time to wipe down any surface that might have his fingerprints. He knew he would be leaving DNA evidence, but his DNA was not in any Western database.

He went outside, put his bag in his car, and moved the vehicle near the exit. He screwed the silencer onto the barrel of his Sig Sauer and walked back into the hotel. He kept the pistol tucked behind his back and covered by his coat.

Jonathan Scanlan was still seated at the bar with his back to the restaurant's entrance. Hai Li stopped when he was ten feet from Scanlan, pulled his gun from behind his back and aimed at the man's heart.

Two quick shots were fired in quick succession.

Jonathan spun around to see a middle-aged Asian man falling to the floor with a surprised expression on his face. Carolyn lowered her gun. One woman screamed and the late diners ran out of the restaurant.

"Like you, I guess, I decided to come down for a drink."

It took several minutes before Jonathan could speak. "Glad you did."

Two uniformed patrolmen were the first to arrive. They entered the restaurant with guns drawn. Carolyn had placed her Glock on the bar. Both policemen glanced at the dead man and pointed their weapons at Jonathan and Carolyn. In unison they shouted, "Put your hands up."

Both Carolyn and Jonathan did so. Carolyn, displaying no emotion, said, "We're feds. We can show you our credentials."

Neither policeman seemed to know what to do. Finally, one said, "Okay, lower your hands slowly and bring out your creds."

"Maybe these are real, and maybe they aren't. Don't move, detectives are on the way."

Twenty long minutes later, two detectives in plain clothes arrived. They examined Carolyn and Jonathan's credentials with a good deal of skepticism.

The older detective said, "Defense Intelligence Agency. Never heard of it."

Neither Jonathan nor Carolyn replied.

"Who shot this man?"

Carolyn said, "I did. The patrolman has my gun."

The younger detective asked, "Why did you shoot him?"

"Because he was about to kill him." She motioned toward Jonathan. "If you look, you'll see a silenced pistol next to the dead man."

Both detectives looked down. The lead detective said, "I'm placing you under arrest and taking you in until this is all straightened out."

Jonathan stared at the lead detective. "Officer, how close are you to retirement?"

The detective's face flushed with anger. "Turn around, asshole, and put your hands behind your back."

They both complied. Carolyn said, "The DIA is part of the Department of Defense. Arresting two of its agents isn't a wise move. We can give you the name and number of the director of our agency."

Several members of the press had joined the looky-loos that had gathered at the entrance to the restaurant. Cameras were running.

Jonathan glanced at the younger detective, who was looking very nervous. "There were several people in here who saw what happened. You'd be smart to talk to them."

The younger detective turned to his partner. "Hal, if what they say is true, they're basically federal cops."

This did make the senior detective pause as he looked over at the cameras. "All right, sit them down. I'll make some calls."

The younger detective, who introduced himself as Detective Brian Gorham, uncuffed them and led them to a nearby table and told them to sit down. He then went over to the woman who had been working at the wine bar and asked her what she had seen.

Twenty minutes later, the senior detective returned. He huddled for a moment with Detective Gorham before approaching Jonathan and Carolyn. "Your story checks out. You're free to go, but you need to come down to our station tomorrow and sign a statement."

Carolyn asked, "Can you give me back my gun?"

The senior detective said, "No." And walked away.

Gorham leaned down and said, "We need to have forensics check it out, but we can give it back to you when you show up for your statement."

As Carolyn and Jonathan were leaving the restaurant, the reporters began shouting out questions. Jonathan smiled and said, "No comment," as they walked toward the elevators.

CHAPTER 54

After a fitful sleep, Jonathan joined Carolyn and Doug for coffee. Apparently, the crime scene people had come and gone. There was no trace of the evening's event.

After they filled Doug in on the shooting, he said, "You guys have all the fun. So, what happens now?"

"Well, we have to go down to police headquarters and make a formal statement. I need to make a few calls. How about we meet in the lobby in an hour?"

When Jonathan returned to his room, he took a moment to again review Frey's phone records. There was one call to a number with a 769-area code. When he dialed it, a male voice with a heavy southern accent said, "You've reached Dion Hart, please leave a message."

Jonathan hung up and dialed the number for NAI UCR Properties and asked to speak to Dion Hart. When the receptionist put through the call, he again hung up.

It was too early to call Cal, but he did reach Myron, who was still staying at Jonathan's home. Everything, including Bo, was fine. He decided to wait until he was home before he told Cal and Myron about the shooting.

When they were in the Explorer, Jonathan handed Doug Detective Gorham's card. Doug entered the address into the navigation system, and after a short drive, they were at the Jackson police headquarters. The building was a one-story structure and could have been mistaken for a low-end office building, had it not been for the sign over the entrance.

Doug went in with Jonathan and Carolyn, but once inside was told to stay in a waiting area while Jonathan and Carolyn made their statements. The senior detective, whose name was Donald Beck, was all smiles and handshakes today. They recorded their statements in less than an hour.

Jonathan asked if they had identified the Asian man. Beck said, "He had an id and credit cards under the name Winston Chow, but we're sure that wasn't his name. So far, he hasn't shown up in any of our databases."

Carolyn said, "Please send what you have to Director Nichols. We have access to international databases."

"Will do."

As they were about to leave, Detective Gorman handed Carolyn her gun. She thanked him and they were out the door.

When they were in the Explorer, Jonathan handed Doug a slip of paper. "What's this?"

"Our next stop."

Doug entered the address on Katherine Drive into the vehicle's GPS system and gave Jonathan a questioning look.

"It's the address of a large real estate company."

Fifteen minutes later, Doug pulled into the parking lot for customers and employees of NAI UCR Properties. The trio stepped out of the SUV and walked into the building. An attractive young woman at the reception desk smiled and asked, "How can I help you?"

Jonathan returned her smile and said, "We'd like to speak with Dion Hart, please."

"Do you have an appointment with Dion?"

"No, I'm sorry, we don't."

"Dion's quite busy. I suggest you call and arrange for an appointment."

Jonathan sighed and presented his DIA credentials. "That's not going to happen. We have some questions for Mr. Hart, and we're not going away."

The flustered receptionist stared at Jonathan and his companions for a moment before picking up her phone and telling Dion Hart that he had visitors.

A few minutes later, a tall black man in his early thirties came into the reception area with a puzzled expression.

"I'm Dion Hart. How can I help you?"

"Mr. Hart, we're from the Defense Intelligence Agency, and we need to ask you a few questions. Is there somewhere we can talk privately?"

Jonathan could tell from Dion Hart's change of expression; he had quickly put two and two together. "Of course, please follow me."

He led them to a small conference room. When they were seated, Jonathan asked, "We only wish to confirm that Robert Frey came to Jackson to see you."

Hart glanced around the room, as if looking for a way out. "Mr. Hart, we're not here to judge you or Mr. Frey. Please answer my question."

Hart's eyes finally settled on Jonathan. "Will this hurt Bob at DOD?"

"No. In fact, it eliminates Mr. Fry from what we're investigating."

"Yes. I met Bob a couple of years ago when I was in DC for a conference and we became friends."

"Thank you for your time, Mr. Hart. We'll see ourselves out."

When they were in Doug's SUV, he turned to Jonathan. "So that's it. Hart is Frey's gay boyfriend?"

"That's it."

Carolyn shook her head. "With Frey off the list, we're back to square one."

CHAPTER 55

It took several days for Beijing to learn that Shadow was no more. While a shooting in Jackson, Mississippi, was not newsworthy, the attempted murder of a federal agent did get picked up by a few media outlets. There was no direct link that could tie Hai Li to Beijing, but there was no question that the people in Washington knew who had employed the assassin.

There was a great deal of discussion regarding how the administration might retaliate. Dong Jun, the Minister of National Defense, concluded that, since Hai Li had been so spectacularly incompetent, there would probably be no retaliation.

Unfortunately for Beijing, Hai Li's failure meant the investigation would continue and their man at the Pentagon was still at risk. Chan Wening, who was still in San Francisco, was demanding a plane load of assassins to finish off Jonathan Scanlan and Cal Hulse.

Jun had already decided that a change at Intelligence was needed. It was apparent Chan Wening had been ineffective and simply did not handle stress well. Such a move would be done quietly when Wening returned to Beijing. He did agree that Scanlan and Hulse needed to be eliminated. Not by a plane load of assassins, but a small elite team drawn from the Jiaolong Commandos. The group, often called the Sea Dragons, was comparable to the United States SEALs.

Jun made the call. The only special criterion was that all the team members would need to be fluent in English. The result was a team of six. None of the team members had ever been to the United States, so a crash course was given on American culture and behavior. Since all six men had short, military-style haircuts, they were instructed to allow their hair to grow longer.

They were given false passports showing they were from Taiwan, Cambodia, and Viet Nam, and they were told to travel in pairs. Two entered the United States through western Canada, two through eastern Canada, and two through Hawaii. The two from eastern Canada were the last to arrive in San Francisco. Apartments had been rented in the city's Chinatown, and local operatives provided the weapons they would use.

Their instructions were to kill Jonathan Scanlan. If Hulse could also be killed, to do so, but Scanlan was the main target. When the mission was completed, the team would drive to Los Angeles, again traveling in pairs, and exit the country.

Chan Wening was kept informed, but it was clear Minister Jun was running the show. The head of Intelligence was, in fact, quite intelligent and was starting to have very bad feelings about his future.

Local operatives were told to keep Scanlan and his home under 24/7 surveillance.

When their investigation of Robert Frey was completed, Carolyn returned to Washington, Doug to Huntsville and Jonathan to San Francisco. After he arrived home and was greeted by Myron and Bo, Jonathan called Cal. After explaining why Robert Frey was not the leaker, he suggested they meet for dinner the next evening and talk about what next steps they should take.

"Sure Jon. Make reservations. You pick the place."

Myron had noticed that the house was again under surveillance and insisted on driving Cal and Jonathan to dinner.

When Cal slid into the back seat of the Lincoln, he turned to Jonathan. "Where are we going?"

"Gary Danko."

"Great choice. I haven't been there in years."

Myron dropped them off at the restaurant's entrance on North Point. When Jonathan asked Myron to join them, he declined, saying he was in the mood for a hamburger. He agreed to pick them up when they were ready to leave.

Cal and Jonathan were seated immediately. When asked, Cal ordered a Belvedere martini while Jonathan went with a glass of Chardonnay. As he took his first sip, Cal said, "Too bad it wasn't Frey. If he were our guy, this whole thing would be over."

Jonathan nodded in agreement. "Yeah, he gave Carolyn a bullshit explanation for his trip to Mississippi because he hasn't come out."

"I have no idea where we go from here."

Jonathan again nodded. "I don't either, and frankly, I'm tired of living like this."

"I agree, but as long as they believe we're still on the case, the risk continues."

"You know, right after I got back, Myron spotted guys watching my house. Have you seen anyone at your place?"

Cal shook his head. "No, but my unit doesn't face the street so we might not know."

"Have Lamar check the street periodically."

"Sure, say, let's talk about something else. While you were gone, one columnist wrote about trading Curry."

"That's crazy, he's still our best player."

When the waiter appeared, Jonathan ordered a small salad, the duck breast and a bottle of Williams Selyem Pinot. Cal went with the medium-rare petite filet with potatoes and cauliflower.

The rest of the conversation over dinner revolved around the two new players the Giants had picked up and the 49ers' most pressing needs. While they did not want to talk about the thousand-pound gorilla in the room, the ongoing threat dominated both men's minds.

When Myron picked them up after dinner, he mentioned the car that followed them home.

CHAPTER 56

Jonathan sat at his desk in his study and brooded over his untenable situation. They were no closer to finding the person leaking classified information to the Chinese than when they started the investigation. The Chinese would continue their attempts to stop the investigation by killing him, Cal, and possibly Cory. It was a nightmare that had no end.

He did not believe stopping the investigation would have any effect on stopping the threat from Beijing. Jonathan was also angry at being their target. He would be dead had it not been for the efforts of Myron and Carolyn.

He was also angry at constantly playing defense. As he mulled over his situation, a thought came to him. He spent the next hour thinking it through before picking up his cell and dialing a number in DC.

It was picked up on the second ring. "Director Nichols, it's Jonathan Scanlan. I have an idea, but to pull it off, I'd need your help."

For the next fifteen minutes, Jonathan pitched his plan. When he finished, there was a pause before the director spoke. "Let me think about it. I'll call you in a day or two."

Later that day, Cal called. "I had Lamar check the street outside my building. You were right, they're back. He said they're using two cars, rotating them every hour or so, trying not to be too obvious."

"Thanks, Cal, try to be careful when you go anywhere."

"You too."

Jonathan had the feeling things were accelerating.

Director Nichols called the following day. "Morning Jonathan. I've given your idea a great deal of thought. There is a high level of risk, but with a few tweaks, I'm willing to go for it. It will take about five days to put everything in place."

Four day later, Jonathan picked up his landline and called Cal. "Hi Cal, why don't you come over to my place for dinner tomorrow night?"

"Great, what time?"

"Why don't you get here about seven?"

"You're on."

———

Jonathan's dinner plans were immediately provided to the Jiaolong Commandos in Chinatown.

The six-man team left their apartments in casual civilian clothes, which hid all traces of their body armor. Their tactics had been carefully worked out and no one spoke as they drove across town to Jackson Street. The silenced Glocks would be used to kill everyone in the house. Their assault weapons would only be employed if there was unexpected resistance.

Each man carried a Glock 10 pistol and a Ruger AR-556 assault rifle. The Glocks were silenced while the AR-556s were not. Each Glock held sixteen rounds, including the one in the chamber. The AR-556s held thirty rounds. All the men had three spare magazines for both weapons.

While these were not the weapons they had trained with, they were not that different from the Type 92 pistols and NP42s they were familiar with. The Chinese-made weapons from Norinco had proved difficult to acquire on short notice.

At eight o'clock, they parked their two vehicles on the quiet street. A battering ram was pulled from the trunk of one of the cars. They silently made their way to the front door. The man with the ram hit the door just below the lock.

The crashing sound of the ram hitting the door and the door flying open echoed through the house. The lead man dropped the battering ram and stepped aside, allowing his teammates to stream into the house.

When the Chinese commandos flooded into the entry, a booming voice shouted, "Drop your weapons." Six heavily armed Seals, who had been behind a low wall bordering the Presidio, had vaulted the wall and raced to the front of the house. Another team of Seals appeared from the living room and stairway leading to the second floor.

The commandos instantly spread out and began firing their assault weapons. Within seconds, all six were down, dropped by withering fire from inside the house and from the team that had been waiting at the edge of the Presidio.

Five of the Chinese commandos were dead. One who had been hit in the leg was thrashing about on the floor, gripping his leg. One of the Navy SEALs had been hit in the arm. Triage was performed on the Seal and the wounded commando.

The SEAL team leader, Lieutenant Commander Charles Howes, stepped out of the living room and studied the carnage. Cal and Jonathan came out of one of the upstairs bedrooms and made their way down the stairs.

Cal's face became pale when he saw the dead men on the floor. All he could say was, "Jesus Christ."

Jonathan approached the SEAL team leader. "It worked."

The man simply nodded.

"I wasn't sure they were still monitoring my landline; obviously, they were."

"It'll be interesting to see what we can get out of the one that's still alive." He paused and looked around. "Sorry about the house getting shot up."

Jonathan waved off the comment. "I wonder if this'll stop them from coming after Cal and me."

The Lieutenant Commander shrugged. "They are a persistent lot, but someone's going to be in deep shit in Beijing."

It took a while for the mess to be cleaned up. The Seals had worn body cameras, so the event was well recorded. The wounded commando was taken away under heavy guard, and the wounded Seal left in a different ambulance. Neighbors had called the police as soon as they heard the gunfire. When the patrol cars arrived, the uniforms had no idea what they should do. Detectives were called in, only to be rebuffed by Howes. They were told that it was a national security matter and no statements would be made. When Lincoln Fenton, the head of the city's detectives, arrived, he was also turned away.

As he walked away, he was glaring at Jonathan and Cal, as this was not their first encounter.

CHAPTER 57

Shortly after the police arrived, the press descended on Jackson Street. They, too, were denied access. A few of the more aggressive members of the fifth estate attempted to push their way into the house, only to be met with forceful resistance by several of the Seals.

Their demands to be given information on the event fell on deaf ears. They were able to use their cameras to record the body bags leaving the house and the wounded leaving in ambulances. As soon as they learned the home's owner was Jonathan Scanlan, a highly successful author, their demands hit new levels. Talking heads with no information immediately popped up on all the television stations, expounding on a variety of speculations, none of which touched on reality.

The inability to be given the details behind the shooting only fueled the media's interest. Reporters and camera crews remained outside Jonathan's home in the hope of waylaying the man and gaining an exclusive. Twice, the police were called to remove reporters who had made their way into the backyard.

Jonathan's movements were more limited than when the Chinese were dogging him. Even Myron was questioned when he left the house to go grocery shopping and do other errands. Given the man's size and the fact that he was armed, the aggressive questioning was limited.

While unhappy to be a shut-in, Jonathan knew the situation was temporary, and he used the time to supervise the repairs to his home. He also felt some satisfaction in having taken action against Beijing's operators. The big question was, would they still come after him when the dust settled?

Beijing and the CCP were mute, refusing to comment on the attack. Their ambassador to the UN mentioned that violence was endemic to the United States.

Chan Wening, who was still in the city, had heard through his contacts that the Minister of National Defense was blaming the debacle on him, even though he had been pushed out of the loop. They were also demanding his return to China.

Wening knew a return to the homeland would greatly shorten his life. He saw only two alternatives for survival. He could turn himself in to the American authorities and ask for political asylum or kill Jonathan Scanlan. While the Americans would certainly welcome the former head of Chinese intelligence, he would have to go into a version of the Witness Protection Program and would remain Beijing's number one target for assassination. Not an appealing option.

If he succeeded in killing Scanlan, Beijing would have to welcome him back. The risks were considerable. He had never been a field operator. He rose in the bureaucracy through his intelligence and the help of several powerful people. The support of those people was certainly wavering, but he was confident that killing Scanlan would turn that around.

He knew he could do nothing while the press was camped out at Scanlan's home, but sooner or later that would end, and the man would expose himself. He just had to have patience.

After five days, the reporters had given up and moved on to the next story. Myron had not seen any sign of surveillance, and Jonathan began cautiously leaving the house. He and Bo resumed running in the Presidio, and with Myron in tow, he would occasionally go to the driving range at Harding. With nothing to do and feeling at loose ends, Jonathan called Cal. As usual, he left a message. Two hours later, his friend called back.

"Hay, Jon. What's happening? Is the press still outside?"

"No, they pulled out a few days ago. How about dinner tomorrow night?"

"Sure, pick the place and let me know."

The following evening, Myron drove Jonathan and Cal to the North Beach Restaurant. They offered to have him join them, but he declined. The place was packed, and it took a little while to get a table.

"Good choice, Jon. Way back when, I used to come here a lot, but I haven't been back in years."

"Same here."

Cal smiled and looked around the restaurant. "I think I just gained five pounds when we walked in."

Jonathan had to laugh. "I agree. Are you back at it, solving problems for the techs?"

"Yeah, DIA is still paying me, but unless something changes, there's nothing for me to do."

"Are you still in touch with Carolyn?"

Cal blushed and offered a sheepish grin. "We talk now and then."

"I know the East Coast, West Coast thing is tough, but I hope things work out."

Jonathan could see that Cal found the direction of the conversation to be uncomfortable. He remembered feeling the same way when he was asked about Cory. To shift the conversation, he asked, "Do you think the Chinese have backed off?"

Cal shrugged. "I don't know. God, I hope so. It would be great to get back to a normal life."

The waiter showed up with their drink orders. As they clinked glasses, Jonathan said, "Here's to better times."

They took a while studying the menu. Cal finally decided on the pasta della casa, and Jonathan ordered the Bucatini all Amatriciano, and a bottle of Italian wine that the waiter recommended.

Over dinner, they talked about which democrat would win the upcoming governor's race in California before shifting to the NFL draft.

While they were enjoying their dinners, Chan Wening was freezing his ass off as he huddled in the doorway of a nearby store that was closed for the night. He had planned to shoot the two men when they left the restaurant, but there were two problems with his plan. The restaurant was on a busy street with pedestrians all over the place, and parking in North Beach was so bad that he had to park three blocks from the restaurant.

He concluded there was no way he could escape after killing the men. He finally gave up on the idea and walked back to his car.

CHAPTER 58

Closed-door meetings became the rule of the day in Beijing. Chan Wening, the now former head of Intelligence, had gone off the grid. He had moved out of his hotel and had not responded to their communications for six days, and his secure phone was no longer active. China had never had a serious defection, while there was no news that Wening had gone over to the other side, the possibility badly frightened the leadership.

The man knew everything. For the first time in his life, the Minister of National Defense doubted he would survive such an event. Several of those close to him were attempting to distance themselves from the potential disaster.

The President of the People's Republic of China was not pleased with the disastrous outcome in San Francisco. While not referring to it as an act of war, the president of the United States had withdrawn the Ambassador to China and threatened to impose serious tariffs on Chinese imports. Beefing up defense support for Taiwan was also being discussed.

In one of the emergency meetings, Dong Jun instructed Chan Wening's replacement and General Qian Huang, Jun's second of command and leader of the army, to find Chan Wening and silence him.

The general stared at the minister. "We cannot use the military after what happened with the commandos."

"No, we cannot." He turned to Ming Sun, Wening's replacement. "I know we have many operatives in the United States. Use them to find Wening."

Sun nodded. "We do. He will be using false papers, so it will not be easy."

Jun slammed his fist on the table and shouted, "It may not be easy, but it must be done."

A badly shaken, newly appointed head of Intelligence gathered his papers and hurried out of the room.

———

Six thousand miles away in San Francisco, Chan Wening sat in his new hotel room as he considered his situation. He knew a major alarm had gone off when he stopped taking their communications and went off the grid. He also knew they would come after him. They knew his last location was San Francisco, but by now, he could be anywhere.

He had excellent identification papers, as well as credit cards issued by US banks under the name Richard Chang, and the people in Beijing were unaware of his new identity.

He also thought about his wife and two children in Beijing and wondered if he would ever see them again. He was loyal to his country and would never betray it, but he also knew how the leadership would react.

Wening had read *The Independence Conspiracy* and, while the outcome had infuriated him, he had to admit that Jonathan Scanlan and Cal Hulse were brilliant and resourceful. They survived several attempts to kill them when they were investigating Independence. While the attempts by the cartel men had been poorly performed, they had taken out Shadow, his country's best assassin. They could not be underestimated.

When he gave it more thought, Hulse and Scanlan had survived these attempts, but neither man had ever fired a shot. He considered that to be remarkable and a bit confusing.

Being incommunicado with the people in Beijing eliminated his information flow regarding Scanlan's movements. Previously, he knew when the man was about to take a trip, where he was going, and his flight information. Even his movements within the city were monitored. None of that was now available.

There was no way he could observe Scanlan twenty-four-seven. He was also not confident he could perform the surveillance without being noticed. After a good deal of thought, he concluded he needed to use technology. Ten minutes on Google, and he found what he needed. Wening drove to an electronics store on Geary that specialized in security systems.

Later that evening, he drove past Jonathan Scanlan's home and noticed there were no vehicles parked outside the house. He was not surprised. The home had a three-car garage. He knew Scanlan owned an older Jeep, and the big man who accompanied him everywhere drove a very large Lincoln.

The following day, Wening was parked a block away from Scanlan's home when the Lincoln pulled out of the garage. He ducked down when the car drove past him. When the Lincoln was well past him, Wening turned his rental around and followed at a comfortable distance. Myron drove to the Marina Safeway, parked in the lot, and walked into the store.

As soon as Myron was inside the supermarket, Wening pulled into a space alongside the big car, stepped out of his car, knelt, and placed a device inside the Lincoln's rear bumper. He quickly got back in his car and drove out of the lot.

He drove a block away and pulled to the side of the road. He turned on the monitor and watched the screen. A half hour later, a dot on the screen began moving. Staying three blocks back from the Lincoln, he followed until he was sure the tracking device was working properly.

After the recent attempts, it appeared that when Jonathan Scanlan left his home, the big man drove him wherever he wanted to go in the Lincoln. Wening now had a method to track the car's movements without having to follow them.

Unfortunately for Chan Wening, wherever Scanlan went, the big man was present, and the man had proved to be an excellent shot.

Wening knew Chinese operatives would be scouring the country, searching for him. While enough time had elapsed for him to be anywhere, San Francisco was his last known location, and he had to assume a great deal of focus would be on the city. To his advantage, San Francisco had the largest concentration of Chinese in the United States, with nearly two hundred thousand residents claiming Chinese ancestry.

His disadvantage was that almost all these people lived in normal residences, not hotels. The people searching for him would certainly focus on the hotels. He went online and looked for furnished apartments for rent. He quickly secured a two-bedroom unit in the Richmond District, an area with a heavy Asian population.

Whenever the Lincolns left the Jackson Street home, Chan Wening would follow, staying several blocks back. Most often, the big man was alone, and Wening would drive away. One day, Lincoln led him to a golf course. Wening's mind raced as he knew Scanlan would be exposed on the open fairways.

Scanlan and the big man stepped out of the car and opened the trunk. The big man pulled out a golf bag and handed it to Scanlan. Chan Wening knew little about the game of golf. His only weapon was a 9mm Sig Sauer pistol, so a long-range shot on the course was not feasible. He doubted he could rent a cart, as he had no clubs and was not dressed for golf.

He decided his best plan would be to sneak onto the course, wait for Scanlan to pass, and shoot him at close range. When Scanlan walked into the clubhouse, Wening left his car and moved across the parking lot. He was passing a row of golf carts and noticed they each had scorecards on their steering wheels. He picked a card off one of the carts and returned to his car.

When he studied the card, he noticed, in addition to the space for recording scores, some information was provided regarding the distances for each hole. He did not see how that information would help him. He opened his laptop and googled the Harding Park Golf Course.

Shooting Scanlan somewhere in the interior of the course was a no-go. He would probably be seen, and he would be a long way from his car. He decided to leave the parking lot and park on Skyline Boulevard, one of the bordering streets.

He was about to leave the lot when the sound of balls being hit caught his attention. Staying out of sight of the big man, who was still sitting in the Lincoln, he moved toward the main building. He approached the sound and found a long row of men and women hitting golf balls into an open field. Jonathan Scanlan was halfway down the row.

Staying well back, he watched Scanlan until the man put the club he had been using back in his golf bag, picked up the bag, and walked away. When Scanlan returned to the Lincoln, the big man opened the trunk, and Scanlan tossed the bag into it. Moments later, the Lincoln drove away.

While disappointed, Wening assumed, sooner or later, Scanlan would actually play a round of golf. When that occurred, his opportunity would come. He also realized he needed to obtain a rifle.

CHAPTER 59

Chan Wening found that obtaining a firearm would require him to complete a good deal of paperwork, which would then be provided to the government. Not something he wanted to happen. His research on Google confirmed that the purchase of a long gun would require it to be registered with the California Department of Justice. A further problem was the ten-day waiting period. That was not going to work.

Working his way up within the Chinese intelligence community had required him to pass periodic firearm tests. He passed the tests, but only barely. He accepted the fact that he was not a very good shot. To kill Scanlan using his Sig Sauer, he would have to be quite close. Shooting him on a golf course at a distance did not appear to be a winning plan.

After the disastrous commando raid on his home, Scanlan was sure to have fortified his house. Wening could not see how he could get to the man in his home. He knew, from early reports, that the man liked to take runs with his dog in the San Francisco Presidio. Wening had no idea what the Presidio was or where it was located. He tried to use Google, but other than learning about the Presidio's history, his search was not helpful.

Wening's next Google search came up with a nearby bookstore. Ten minutes later he was in Green Apple Books on Clement. A helpful clerk guided him to a section of the store that offered maps. He eventually found one that had a detailed map of the city, including the Presidio.

The man studied the map for some time. While it was helpful, it was not enough. He had to go to the area and see it for himself. He did not have any hiking apparel, but he did have casual clothing. What he did not have were shoes that would work.

On The Run was the closest athletic shoe store. A short drive across Golden Gate Park brought him to the shop on Taraval Street. He had never purchased athletic shoes and had no idea what his shoe size would be in America.

An overly helpful sales clerk questioned him about whether he was a runner or a walker and what type of surfaces he ran or walked on. He faked a few answers and was finally able to leave the store with a pair of Nikes.

It was mid-afternoon when Wening parked on Pacific Avenue, several blocks away from Scanlan's home on Jackson. He went into the Presidio and stayed on paths on the south side of the national park. When he believed he was near the area of the park across from Scanlan's home, he began studying the area. There were several areas near the path where he could be concealed. Of course, he had no idea if Scanlan used this particular path. He also did not know when the man ran. He really did not want to spend days hiding in the bushes, hoping the man would run by.

Wening was becoming increasingly frustrated. Killing the man should not be this difficult. The problem was the big man. Wherever Scanlan went, he was accompanied by the big man, except when he went for a run.

As he drove away from the Presidio, a thought came to him. Most people were creatures of habit. They tended to get up in the morning at the same time and go to bed at the same time. They ate their meals at the same time. Their routines were fairly predictable. He wondered if Jonathan Scanlan's runs followed a pattern. Events could cause variations, but if the man tended to run at nearly the same time, killing him might be easily accomplished.

Of course, he had to find out if such a pattern existed. He knew that when the cartel men attacked him, Scanlan had been going for a run in the afternoon. Wening decided he would park his car at least two blocks from the man's home in the afternoon for a few days to see if there was a pattern to his runs.

The following day, Wening arrived at one in the afternoon and sat in his rental with a view of Scanlan's street. The weather was cold, but the sky was clear. He had brought along a thermos of tea to keep himself alert. There was no sign of Scanlan, and at six o'clock he drove away.

The next day, he repeated his vigil. At a little after three, he saw Scanlan and his dog cross the street and enter the park. An hour later, the man and dog left the park, walked across the street, and went into their home.

On day three, Scanlan did not go for a run. The following day, at 2:30, Scanlan and his dog again crossed into the park for their run. Slightly over an hour later, they left the Presidio and went home. Wening had his pattern.

Two days later, Chan Wening watched Scanlan and his dog enter the park. He moved his car closer to where Scanlan had walked into the park. Thirty minutes later, he stepped out of his car and went into the Presidio. He found some heavy cover ten yards from where Scanlan and the dog would walk out of the park. He crouched down and waited. He had never killed anyone before, and his nerves were on edge. He wondered if the dog would attack him, and the possibility made him sweat.

He took deep breaths, trying to calm himself. Wening kept telling himself that in a few minutes his problems would be over. Fifteen minutes later, he heard the sound of someone approaching.

CHAPTER 60

Myron was always uneasy when Jonathan went for his runs. His routine was to step out of the house and check the street before Jonathan and Bo took off. When he did so today, there were no suspicious cars parked near the house.

A short time after Jonathan had left, Myron was in the living room and noticed a car had parked across the street. The memory of the attempt on Jonathan by the cartel men flashed through his mind.

When it was approaching the time when Jonathan would be finishing his run, Myron stepped out of the house and crossed the street. He walked several yards into the park when he saw Jonathan.

Jonathan stopped short when he saw Myron. "What's happening?"

"Probably nothing. Someone parked their car across from the house and I wanted to make sure everything was okay."

"Thanks. I'm sure it's nothing. Come on, let's go in and have a beer."

Myron glanced around before turning and leading the way back to the house.

Wening was so nervous he thought he might throw up. He waited half an hour after the two men had gone into the house before emerging from his cover. He quickly walked to his car and drove away. On the drive back to his apartment, he decided it was time to turn in his car and rent a different vehicle.

While Wening was frustrated that he had not been able to kill Scanlan today, he took comfort in now knowing the man's behavior pattern. There was no question that Scanlan was most exposed when he went running. There had to be a time when the big man was not around. Wening decided to continue lying in wait on the days Scanlan went for his run.

Jonathan and Myron had just finished dinner when the doorbell rang. No visitors were expected, so Myron moved to the door holding his Glock. When he peered at the security screen that covered the home's entrance, he motioned to Jonathan and stepped away.

Jonathan opened the door to find Cory standing before him. Neither spoke for a moment.

Finally, Cory broke the silence. "Can I come in?"

For a moment, Jonathan simply stared at her. Not at all sure what was happening, finally he said, "Of course."

Myron turned to the stairs and went up to his room. Without speaking, Jonathan led Cory into the living room. "Can I get you anything, water, coffee, a glass of wine?" The question sounded hollow, even to his own ears.

"No, thank you."

Jonathan took a seat across from her and said nothing.

After a moment of silently staring at each other, Cory said, "We need to talk."

A range of emotions swirled through Jonathan's mind. Was she here to try to resume the relationship, or to formally end it? While he hoped it was the former, her refusal to take his calls gave him pause. Her body was tense as she leaned forward in her chair.

"I've tried to talk to you, so why now?" He failed to hide the note of irritation in his voice.

"I know. I'm sorry. I had a great deal to think about."

Jonathan did not know what to say. Bo came into the room and sat by Jonathan, seeming to sense that there was a great deal of tension in the room.

"Jonathan, I love you, but I can't live with the violence that seems to surround you."

After a moment, Jonathan nodded. "I understand. I never wanted to put you in harm's way."

"I know." A tear ran down Cory's cheek. "I thought it was all over when Independence was exposed, but it wasn't."

"Yes, I know. Is this the last time I'll see you?"

Cory began crying heavily. "I don't know Jonathan." She stood and stumbled across the room and out the door.

Jonathan sat for several minutes, absorbing what she had said. He was no clearer about his future with Cory Bishop than before she had arrived.

The following day, a storm system had moved into the area, ruling out any plans to hit balls or go for a run. Jonathan was restless. The prior evening's conversation with Cory kept running through his mind. In many ways, it would have been easier if she had said that she never wanted to see him again.

He picked up a new book by Grisham, but put it down after a few pages, finding it difficult to concentrate. The investigation was going nowhere, and, like his situation with Cory, he had no idea what to do about it.

Jonathan was pacing the floor when Cal called. "Jon, Carolyn is out here on assignment for a few days and wants to get together."

"Great. Is she staying with you?"

There was a pause. "No, we're not at that point. She's staying at the Hilton on Kearny."

"What do you want to do, lunch, dinner?"

"She's attending a conference during the day, so dinner."

"If I remember right, she was more seafood than red meat. How about the Waterbar?"

"Good place."

"I'll make reservations. Would seven work?"

"Sure," Jonathan noted the upbeat tone in his friend's voice.

"Myron and I'll pick you up. Should we plan to pick Carolyn up?"

"No, she'll meet us there."

While it was not exactly an answer to his problems, it gave him something to do and he looked forward to seeing Carolyn. He picked up the phone and booked a table.

CHAPTER 61

Myron dropped Cal and Jonathan off a few minutes early, and they were immediately led to a table with a view of the bay. Carolyn arrived fifteen minutes later and, after giving Jonathan an awkward hug, she slid into her seat next to Cal.

Jonathan smiled as he noticed the change in Carolyn's appearance. While she previously seemed to downplay her appearance, tonight her hair was perfectly styled, and her black dress complemented her figure. He wondered if there was a Glock in her stylish purse.

When the waiter arrived for drink orders, Carolyn went with a Stoli martini, a far departure from her usual club soda with lime. Cal ordered a French Seventy-Five and Jonathan a glass of Chardonnay.

After a period of chitchat over what was going on in Washington, Jonathan asked, "Has DIA been able to make any progress toward finding the leaker?"

Carolyn frowned and shook her head. "No, and it's driving everyone crazy."

"Well, we haven't come up with anything either."

Carolyn glanced out the window toward the now darkened bay before turning back to Jonathan. "You know what's weird? For them to try so hard to take us out, they had to believe we were close, but I don't see it."

Neither Jonathan nor Cal spoke for a minute. Cal was the first to surface. "You're right, it doesn't make any sense."

Jonathan stared at her for a moment. "Maybe we missed something."

Cal said, "Maybe, but I don't know what the hell it could be."

Jonathan decided to try to shift the conversation and lift the mood. "Cal said you'll be out here for a few days."

"Yes, the conference wraps up on Friday, but I was thinking about using a few vacation days and staying a little longer." As she said this, she glanced at Cal.

He was able to mumble, "Great news."

Jonathan was thinking, this woman has an agenda. "Any plans for what you want to do in your free time?"

Carolyn smiled sweetly and said, "A few."

Cal was saved by the bell when the waiter came to take their orders. Jonathan ordered a butter lettuce salad and red wine-braised short ribs. Carolyn went with the little gem salad and the Dorade, while Cal ordered the same order as Jonathan, who also ordered a bottle of the Frank Family Chardonnay.

While they were waiting for the check, Jonathan called Myron for the ride home. When the Lincoln arrived, Carolyn and Cal slid into the back while Jonathan joined Myron up front. As Myron drove to the Hilton, Jonathan was aware of a little activity in the back seat.

Carolyn was smiling when she stepped out of the car and walked into her hotel. Jonathan turned and looked at his friend as Myron drove out of the entrance area.

"Care to share Carolyn's plans for her free time?"

A thoroughly flustered Cal Hulse turned away and did not provide an answer.

———

Chan Wening had followed the Lincoln, using his tracking device. He had no plan to try to take out Hulse and Scanlan while the big man was around. He found it interesting to see the woman join them when they left the restaurant. His first thought was that she might be a prostitute, but that idea was dismissed when they dropped her off at the Hilton.

He thought she might have replaced Cory Bishop as part of their investigation, but he did not see any way she would be useful to his plan to kill Scanlan.

The forecast was for two more days of rain, which, he assumed, meant Scanlan would not be going for his run. As soon as the rains stopped, he planned to return to his spot in the Presidio.

———

The search for Chan Wening was going nowhere, which was frustrating the Beijing leadership. There had been several false starts; in one case, an overly zealous operative had killed a man in New York, thinking the man was Wening. His picture had been widely distributed but unfortunately, there are many mid-forty, medium build, medium height Asian men in America. The fact that he spoke English without an accent and could easily blend into society did not help.

It also appeared that he had enough funds to travel and live while on the run. It was suggested that they bring in his wife and children and threaten to kill them if he did not return. Unfortunately, since there was no way to communicate those threats to the man, they had no value.

CHAPTER 62

After one night at the Hilton, Carolyn had moved into Cal's condo, ostensibly to save money. Jonathan had to laugh at Cal's feeble attempt to explain the situation. There was little question about Carolyn's game plan. While Cal seemed a bit confused, he also seemed to be enjoying every minute of it.

Two nights later, Jonathan hosted a dinner for Cal, Carolyn, Myron, and himself. Given Carolyn's lack of affinity for red meat, Jonathan had prepared a fennel and dry goat cheese salad with lemon vinaigrette and perciatelli with anchovies and breadcrumbs. Dessert was a store-bought peach pie. Frank Family Chardonnay was served with the salad, and a King Estate Pinot from Willamette Valley with the main course.

Halfway through the main course, Carolyn sat back and said, "My God, how did you learn to cook like this?"

Jonathan had to smile. "I found I really enjoy cooking. I just follow what it says to do in the cookbooks."

"There's more to it than that. If you ever stop writing and investigating, you could open a restaurant."

"Thanks for the compliment, but I prefer to just cook for my friends."

As they finished the main course, Carolyn looked up at Jonathan. "Cal and I were wondering if, after what happened here, the threat would be over."

Jonathan shrugged. "One would think so. They're paying a heavy price diplomatically."

Cal joined in. "So, we can send Myron, Lamar, and Jim home?"

Myron glanced around the table. "I think we should wait a little longer."

Jonathan thought for a moment. "I don't believe Cory still needs protection. She was never the primary target and, if they've been paying attention, they must know she's no longer involved." Jonathan's expression clouded over.

Cal said, "I'm sorry, Jon."

Carolyn smiled as she looked at Jonathan. "Cal said you like to go running in the Presidio."

Jonathan was happy with the shift in the conversation. "Yes, I do."

"I haven't been able to exercise while I've been out here." A comment that made Cal blush. "Could I join you on a run?"

"Of course. The rain's supposed to stop tonight. How about tomorrow? I usually go out around three."

"Look forward to it."

Later, after Carolyn and Cal had left, Jonathan turned to Myron, "Unless Cory feels she wants to keep him around, send JS home."

The next day, Carolyn arrived just before three, dressed in shorts, a Rolling Stones tee shirt, and running shoes. Her hair was pulled back in a ponytail. Jonathan, who was similarly attired, pointed to the shirt and smiled. "Stones fan?"

"Of course, I've seen them three times."

"Great. Well, let's get going. By the way, Bo always runs with me."

"Sure."

Jonathan led the way out of the house, across the street, and into the Presidio. They began running at a modest pace as they warmed up. They ran in single file on the narrow paths, with Jonathan and Bo leading the way. After about ten minutes, Jonathan picked up the pace. He noticed Carolyn had no trouble keeping up.

———

Chan Wening slipped into the park and made his way to his concealed position. He glanced at his watch, knowing it would be nearly an hour before Scanlan finished his run and started to leave the Presidio. As the time for Scanlan to appear neared, his nerves began to tighten. He tried deep breathing, but the exercise offered little help. He kept telling himself that at ten yards, he could not miss.

As they approached the end of their run, Bo became agitated and began barking. Carolyn told Jonathan to stand back as she pulled a pistol from her fanny pack. Realizing things were not going as planned, Wening quietly slipped out of his concealment and moved away from Jonathan and Carolyn.

Keeping her gun pointed ahead, Carolyn slowly moved into the heavy cover. Jonathan stood with Bo, unsure what he should do. Carolyn came back and returned her gun to her fanny pack.

"Someone was back there. They're gone, but it looks like they were there for a while."

"We have a lot of homeless in the city. Maybe it was one of them."

Carolyn was unconvinced. "Maybe, maybe not. Do you always leave the park this way?"

Jonathan nodded. "Sure, we're right across the street from my house."

"If you're going to keep running in the Presidio, I suggest you vary where you enter and leave the park."

Given his recent experiences, he decided to take the woman's advice.

CHAPTER 63

While Cal Hulse's social life had certainly perked up dramatically, Jonathan's life remained on hold. Following Carolyn's advice, he went running on a more erratic schedule and in different areas of the park. He wanted to play golf, but accepted that the exposure was too great.

He was also frustrated that there was no progress in identifying the leaker. He was sure they were missing something. He spent hours studying the information on the aides and staff.

One morning, he sat up in bed as an idea came to him. After scrambling out of bed and into the shower, he called Cal and asked him to call him back. Later that morning, his friend returned his call.

"Jon, has something come up?"

"I had a thought. You know the Chinese reacted when the fake brief went to Kelly, Farrell, and Hardy, so we looked at their aides and staffers. Why don't we go back and ask the three officers about their people?"

Cal thought for a moment. "Jon, don't you think they would have done something if they thought one of their people was the leaker?"

Jonathan sighed. "You're right. I guess I was just grabbing at straws."

"I know, it's frustrating."

"It's beyond frustrating; it's driving me crazy. We have no answers, but we have to keep worrying about getting whacked because the Chinese think we're making progress."

"You think they're still coming after us?"

"Maybe, did Carolyn tell you what happened on our run?"

"Yeah. She said you thought whoever it was might be a homeless guy."

"When's she going back to DC?'

"In two days."

"Well, let's try to get together before she takes off."

"How about tomorrow night?"

"Sure, dinner at my place?"

"Wonderful. About seven?"

"That'll work. I noticed, when we were traveling, Carolyn tends not to order meat."

"Don't worry about it. Last night we had hamburgers."

Happy to have something to do besides thinking about the investigation, Jonathan began planning the dinner. After reviewing several of his cookbooks, he settled on a crunchy mango and avocado salad, roast beef with a shallot and black bean sauce, and garlic mashed potatoes. Dessert would be an array of Häagen-Dazs ice cream flavors. Knowing Myron would be lost looking for several of the salad's ingredients, Jonathan decided to do the shopping while Myron pushed the cart and watched his back.

It took three stops to collect everything he needed.

When Cal and Carolyn arrived, Jonathan was well organized and able to enjoy the group's company for pre-dinner cocktails. Carolyn told Jonathan and Myron about outings she and Cal had taken around the Bay Area, including walking across the Golden Gate Bridge.

Jonathan smiled as he toasted his friends. "I guess it's now Cal's turn to get a tour of DC."

Cal's face slightly reddened. "We've talked about that."

Knowing Carolyn would not be interested, Jonathan and Cal did not go into their usual back-and-forth about the local teams. Myron chipped in and told some amusing stories about his encounters with some of the Hollywood types.

At one point, Jonathan excused himself to take care of last-minute tasks in the kitchen. He returned and guided his guests into the dining room. Jonathan poured Frank Family Chardonnay, his obvious favorite, with the salad.

Carolyn made a little moaning noise as she finished her first bite. "Jonathan, this is incredible. I've never had anything like this."

"It's called crunchy mango and avocado."

"I'd love to have the recipe."

"I'll give Cal a copy."

When the roast beef and mashed potatoes were served, it was Myron who made the moaning sound. A Pine Ridge cab accompanied the main course. While Carolyn was not a big red meat eater, there was nothing left on her plate, and the array of ice creams was also a big hit.

Coffee was served as they sat around the table,

Cal said, "Jon, you've outdone yourself."

Jonathan smiled as he glanced around the table. "It's great to be with friends."

As Cal and Carolyn were on the way out, Cal turned back to Jonathan. "I told Myron to let Lamar go home."

"You think that's wise?"

"I do. I believe the Chinese have backed off after what happened here."

"I hope you're right."

CHAPTER 64

It was midday, and Jonathan was bored and frustrated. The investigation had hit a wall, yet he had no idea if he was still at risk. With nothing else to do, he decided to go for a run. Bo perked up when he saw Jonathan emerge from his bedroom in shorts, a T-shirt, and running shoes.

Myron looked up from a book he had been reading. "Are you going to follow Carolyn's advice and change where you usually enter and leave the park?"

Jonathan shrugged. "I guess so."

"I'll drive you there in the Lincoln."

"That's okay, Bo and I'll use the Jeep."

"Jonathan, at least let me pretend to be protecting you."

After a moment of indecision, Jonathan said, "All right, but we'll take the Jeep. It's easier with Bo."

A few minutes later, Jonathan, Myron, and Bo were on their way.

Myron drove several blocks to the east, finally turning left on Laurel. He then parked on Pacific, across from the Presidio. When Jonathan and Bo went into the park, Myron returned to his book.

Jonathan found that one of the benefits of his runs was that it tended to clear his mind. He and Bo were near the halfway mark when suddenly a name jumped into his head: Joseph Wu. He slowed his pace as his mind tracked what he knew about the young man. A brilliant mind, aide to General Kelly, and the tragic death of his parents. As he turned back toward his Jeep, other thoughts came to mind: the anomaly of a basically average student becoming a brilliant one, a gifted wide receiver who then had no interest in sports, and the inability to contact the man's aunt and uncle.

When he reached the Jeep, he hurriedly put Bo in the back and told Myron, I need to get back to the house."

Myron said nothing, but quickly drove them home.

Once in the house, he called Cal. He left a message, asking for a quick callback. He had just stepped out of the shower and was toweling off when Cal returned the call.

"Jon, are you all right?"

"I'm fine, but we need to spend more time checking out Jonathan Wu."

"Jonathan Wu?"

"He's an aide to General Kelly. There are things about him that bother me."

"Okay, I remember him now. Let me put together everything we have on him. When do you need it?"

"Yesterday." Jonathan hung up and called Carolyn.

When she answered, Jonathan said, "You remember Jonathan Wu?"

"Of course."

"I want to take a harder look at him."

There was a pause before Carolyn said, "All right."

"I'm going to go back to Dallas."

"When?"

"As soon as Cal puts together everything we know about the man."

Carolyn could hear the urgency in Jonathan's voice. "Should I join you?"

Jonathan thought for a moment. "That's probably not necessary. This may not amount to anything."

"If you change your mind, call me."

After he got dressed, he went into his office and began making reservations for his trip.

CHAPTER 65

Cal dropped off a thin file containing everything they knew about Joseph Wu. When Myron learned about Jonathan's upcoming trip, he insisted on coming along.

"I don't think that's necessary. I just need to do more digging into this guy's background."

"Jonathan. People have been trying to kill you on these trips."

"Thanks, Myron, I'll be okay."

"Jonathan, I'm going with you if I have to pay my own way."

Jonathan did not want to argue the point. "All right, I'll call the dog sitter."

The following day, Myron drove them to the airport in the Lincoln. Chan Wening, who had been parked three blocks from Jonathan's house, watched the Lincoln leave on his monitor. He assumed it was going to be another innocuous outing but pulled away from the curb and followed at a distance. His interest piqued when he realized they were leaving the city.

When the Lincoln pulled into the short-term parking area at SFO, he followed, parking his rental forty yards away. Keeping his distance, he watched them enter terminal three in the area covered by United Airlines.

Staying as far away from Myron and Jonathan as possible, Wening purchased a round-trip ticket to Los Angeles, allowing him to follow the two men into the secure area of the airport. With twenty people between them, he shuffled through the TSA security stations.

While they were in line, Jonanthan asked Myron, "Is your gun going to be a problem?"

"It wasn't the last time we flew to Texas."

This time it was a problem. He was pulled aside as his permit was studied.

When Jonathan approached, the TSA official waved him away. Jonathan presented his DIA credentials and said, "He's with me."

This caused a huddle among the TSA people. Eventually, they were waved through.

Wening had left his pistol in his car and breezed through the checkpoint. He had to stall and stay out of sight until Myron's gun issue was resolved. He then followed them through the airport to the gate for the Dallas flight.

He then went back through the airport to the United ticket desk and purchased a one-way ticket to Dallas.

He returned to his apartment and began making plans for his trip. The problem was his gun. He could not take it on the plane, and he no longer had contacts that he could use to obtain a weapon in Dallas.

After a few minutes of thought, he went out and bought a heavy metal, medium-sized container. He broke his gun down and wrapped each piece in heavy aluminum foil, and then each component was wrapped in some clothing. The gun components went into the metal container, which then went into a thick cardboard box.

His next trip was to FedEx. He paid for the package to be shipped overnight to himself at the Marriott in Dallas. He was counting on Scanlan staying at the hotel he had used before. If he was wrong, he might be taking a wasted trip.

———

It was early evening when Jonathan and Myron reached their hotel, too late to do any digging into Wu's background. After checking in and dropping their bags off in their rooms, they went downstairs to the bar in the Centric restaurant.

After drinks were ordered and served, Myron turned to Jonatan. "All right, we're here. Where do we go next?"

"I want to revisit Joseph Wu's high schools."

Myron nodded and did not question what Jonathan was looking for.

———

Chan Wening was able to change his ticket to the red-eye flight leaving at 9:00 pm and arriving in Dallas at 5:00 am. He rented a car at the Dallas airport and, with no traffic at this early hour, he was at the Marriott in an hour.

When he checked in, he smiled at the clerk. "I'm meeting a friend. Has Jonathan Scanlan already checked in?"

The clerk checked his computer. "Yes, he has."

Wening had a silent sigh of relief as he took his room key and walked to the elevators. He assumed wherever Scanlan was planning to go, he probably would not leave the hotel before 8:00 in the morning. He decided to grab a couple of hours' sleep before looking for the man.

The hotel wake-up call came at 7;20. He took a quick shower, dressed, and went downstairs. He purchased two coffees to go and went outside and sat in his rental. If his gun was not discovered by FedEx, it should be arriving sometime during the day.

CHAPTER 66

Jonathan and Myron met in the hotel restaurant at 8:00. Jonathan stayed with his routine, ordering coffee and orange juice. Myron went with the hearty breakfast: eggs, bacon, hash-browns, and coffee.

They were at Marcus High School by 9:30. Myron stayed in the car as Jonathan walked into the administration building. He was directed to the school library, which. With the exception of the librarian, it was completely empty.

The woman gave Jonathan a curious look. "How can I help you?"

"I'd like to see the yearbooks for 2012, 2013, and 2014."

"Can I ask why?"

"Yes, you can ask, but I'm sorry I can't answer." Jonathan showed her his credentials.

"Oh my, this is exciting. Come with me."

She led Jonathan to a bookcase where she pulled down three yearbooks and placed them on one of the tables. "There you are."

Jonathan thumbed through each yearbook until he found photos of Joseph Wu. I addition to the standard school photos, Wu was in a couple of pictures in his football uniform. Jonathan spent several minutes studying the photos, then, using his cell phone, he snapped shots of each yearbook photo.

He thanked the woman, left the library, and joined Myron in the car.

———

Chan Wening had followed Myron and Jonathan to the high school. He was well aware of what happened to Joseph Wu. He wanted to contact Dong Jun and push the panic button, but he no longer had his secure phone. He had discarded it, believing they could locate him through the device. He also thought that if he called the Chinese embassy and told them what was happening, he would probably not live to see the end of the day.

He had no doubt that Scanlan's next stop would be to Memorial High School in Frisco. He drove quickly back to the Marriott and was relieved to find his package had arrived. He took it to his room and tore it open. He assembled the pistol and raced back to his car.

Traffic was irritatingly slow as he drove through the city.

It took Myron an hour and a half to drive from Flower Mound to Frisco, having to again navigate across Dallas. Myron waited in the car while Jonathan went into the school. Jonathan was directed to the school library, where he asked to see the 2015 yearbook. He went through it twice, but found no picture of Joseph Wu.

He sat back in his chair and thought that there were a number of valid explanations why the young man's picture was not in the yearbook. He could have been sick or had some other conflict on the day photos were taken. But it was another question to be answered.

He stepped out of the library and called Cal, leaving a message and telling him he needed an urgent call back.

Surprisingly, Cal's call came ten minutes later.

"Jon, have you found something?"

"Maybe. Can you send me a copy of Joseph Wu's driver's license when he was sixteen and his current driver's license?"

"I'm on it. Give me fifteen minutes."

———

Wening pulled into the Memorial High School lot and parked thirty yards from Myron's car. He was surprised that they were still there. The visit to Marcus High School had only taken about thirty minutes. About twenty minutes later, he watched as Jonathan Scanlan jogged out of the building.

There was no question, the man had figured it out. Wening grabbed his gun in panic and moved quickly toward Myron and the rental. When he was fifteen yards behind the car he fired through the car's rear window at the back of Myron's head.

CHAPTER 67

It was a basic element of Myron's job to be aware of his surroundings, often called situational awareness. When the man stopped behind his car and began bringing up his gun, Myron opened the car's door and rolled out onto the pavement.

Chan Wening, believing he had just killed the big man, moved around the car for an open shot at Jonathan. Before he could fire, Myron, still lying on the ground, fired three quick shots, all hitting Wening in his torso.

The man went down like a puppet whose strings had been cut.

Knowing what would happen next, Myron placed his Glock on the hood of his rental. Jonathan stood like a deer in the headlights, twenty yards from the car. He only moved forward when Myron placed his gun down.

His voice was shaky when he asked, "Are you all right?"

Myron just nodded. They could hear a dozen sirens approaching the school. Apparently, the police assumed they were rushing to another school shooting. Jonathan took out his credentials and held them up as the first patrol cars screeched into the parking lot.

A dozen guns were pointed at Jonathan and Myron as he shouted, "I'm a federal agent and this man is working for me." No one lowered their guns. Finally, two men in suits got out of an unmarked car and approached.

"Keep your hands up." Jonathan and Myron did so as they were patted down.

The lead detective said, "Let me see those credentials." He took a great deal of time studying them. "I've never heard of the Defense Intelligence Agency. What is it?"

"It's part of the Department of Defense. Can I call the people I report to?"

"For all I know, your *credentials* are bullshit. Who killed that man?"

Myron said, "I did, after he shot at me. Check out the car and his gun." He pointed to the shattered windshield.

"Tell you what, we're all going to go downtown and sort this out." Jonathan was placed in the back of Detective Gerald Reidy's unmarked while Myron was put in the back of one of the patrol cars. Neither man was handcuffed.

They kept Jonathan and Myron separated and placed in different interrogation rooms. Reidy was the senior detective and took the lead as he began questioning Jonathan.

"People are calling this agency you say you're with, so, if you're lying, it's not going to stand up for long."

Not new to this experience, Jonathan remained silent.

"Who is the dead guy?"

"I don't know. I never saw him before. Detective, I'm involved in an investigation. Much of what you want to know is classified. I suggest you talk to John Nichols who's the director at DIA."

Reidy stared at Jonathan, his expression beyond skeptical. "What's your relationship with the big guy?"

"Myron Rossi is a private investigator, and he was there to protect me."

Reidy slammed his fist on the table. "You say you're with this agency, but have a pi for protection? If you needed protection, why wasn't it being provided by this DIA outfit. What you're saying makes no sense."

Jonathan did not respond.

After a few more questions that Jonathan did not answer, the interrogation room door opened and the detective who had been with Reidy at the scene stepped into the room.

"He's a fed."

Detective Reidy, who had been standing, sat down in one of the chairs. "So, that's it? He and his friend can just walk out of here?" Reidy's face was flushed with anger.

"They'll both have to give us a statement, yeah."

After several minutes of silently fuming, he said, "All right, Callejo. Get together with Mary and take their statements."

An hour later Jonathan and Myron walked out of the station. Jonathan took out his phone and ordered an Uber ride.

Neither man spoke until they were back at the Marriott. Once inside, Jonathan said, "Let's go to my room. We need to talk to Nichols."

Jonathan dialed the man's number and the director picked up on the first ring.

"Jonathan, you've had a busy day."

"You can say that, Director. I know who is leaking our stuff to the Chinese. It's an aide to General Kelly named Joseph Wu."

The director was silent for a moment. He finally asked, "How do you know it's him?"

"Because he's not Joseph Wu. They must have killed Joseph Wu when his family was killed. This guy then became Wu. It was quite clever. Both young men were about the same age and had a somewhat similar appearance, but there were differences. Joseph was a good student, but not remarkable. The new guy is brilliant. Joseph was really good at sports; the new guy is not athletic. But the clincher is, Joseph Wu was five feet eleven inches tall when he was a junior in high school, the new guy is five feet eight."

"Jesus, why didn't we pick that up?"

"Sir, it's not something you'd normally be looking for."

"Have a good trip home. I'll be in touch."

Jonathan looked up at Myron, who had been staring at him. "Let's go downstairs and have a drink. We can go home tomorrow."

CHAPTER 68

Jonathan sat at his desk and thought about all that had happened. The investigation ended up being successful, but at a price. It had cost him his relationship with Cory. On a personal level, the only bright spot was that the threat to him and to his friends was over.

Cal had been amused when he learned the breakthrough was the difference in height between the two men.

Myron and the Lincolns had gone back to Southern California, where he would need to buy more Glocks. Jonathan thought about how many times the big man had saved his life. He felt he had to do more than say, thank you and give him a check. Jonathan knew Myron was renting an apartment in Glendale, and he decided, as a bonus for having kept him alive, he would buy Myron a home.

With nothing else to do, he had started making notes for his next book. Jonathan wondered what details the DIA would be objecting to.

His phone chirped, and a glance at the screen showed that it was Director Nichols.

"Hello, Director."

"Morning, Jonathan. I thought you'd like to know. The man posing as Joseph Wu is in custody and is being quite cooperative. As a result, we also have his handler."

"Is there going to be a trial?"

"I don't believe so. We tend to keep these things quiet. Maybe a prisoner swap for one of our people. From what I hear, the young man seems to want to stay here, rather than go back to China."

Jonathan wondered if keeping it quiet meant problems for his future book. "Any word on the man Myron Rossi shot?"

This brought out a chuckle from the director. "The man's name is Chan Wening. He was the head of the Chinese intelligence services."

Jonathan began thinking about the retaliation that might be coming down the road. "Will they be coming after Myron and me?"

"No, not at all. Our information is that he had already been booted out of office and Beijing had operatives after him. I mentioned to you earlier that we have another leak, either at the White House or State. Would you like to get involved?"

"I appreciate the offer, but I'm looking forward to some downtime."

"I totally understand. Well, job well done. If you ever need anything, give me a call."

When the call ended, Jonathan called Cal and left a message, asking if he'd like to meet for dinner."

His second call was to Myron, who answered on the first ring. "Myron, I just received a call from Nichols. Do you know who you shot?"

When Myron did not answer, Jonathan said, "The guy had been the head of China's version of the CIA."

"Does this mean I'm in deep dodo?

"No, Myron. I think Director Nichols wants to give you a medal."

Jonathan was smiling as he hung up.

THANK YOU READER

Thank you for reading, and I sincerely hope you enjoyed my book. As an independently published author, I rely on you the reader to spread the word. So if you enjoyed the book please tell your friends and family, and if it isn't too much trouble, I would appreciate a brief review. They help authors out. Thanks again.

My best to you and yours.

Barry

ABOUT THE AUTHOR

Barry Solloway was born and raised in San Francisco. He has also lived in Los Gatos and Marin. He now lives in Napa with Champ, his chocolate lab, where he's close to his two daughters, Amanda and Kate.

To his mother's great discomfort, Barry as a teenager, worked four summers as an ordinary seaman in the merchant marine, and two summers at casinos in Nevada. He took a year off between achieving his bachelors and masters degrees and hitchhiked throughout Europe.

After doing his service in the Army, he managed businesses in Silicon Valley. He now writes and enjoys all that Napa Valley has to offer.

ALSO BY BARRY SOLLOWAY

Who's Killing the Liberals: Book 1 of the Jonathan Scanlan Series

Secrets: Book 2 of the Jonathan Scanlan Series

The American Dream